# OF WITCHES...

STEVE STRED

Foreword by
MIRANDA CRITES

BVP

Foreword and artwork by Miranda Crites

Cover by vergvoktre

Lettering by Mason McDonald

Formatting by Ross Jeffery

# TABLE OF CONTENTS

x- Foreword by Miranda Crites

1 - In Waves

10 - A Cave, In the Woods

26 - Grandma's Letters

40 - Three Words

52 - The Witch

114 - The Tree (The Witch 2)

130 - Won't You Open the Door?

158 - The Assistant

# FOREWORD

I first met Steve Stred online in 2018. We connected on multiple social media platforms and soon became friends. At that point, Steve already had quite a few books out. I started reading his work, and it didn't take long to realize that this man is quite talented. I was on top of the world when he asked me to beta read for him.

Fast-forward a couple years, and we pretty much communicate on a daily basis. I've done artwork and photography for him, which was included in "The Boy Whose Room Was Outside," and in return, Steve sent me a signed copy of one of his books. He even created an e-book collection of stories especially for me. I still fangirl over things like that. I was ecstatic when Steve asked for more artwork and photography for his new collection. I hope the fluttery feeling I get in my stomach and chest over getting an opportunity to work in the book world never goes away.

When Steve first contacted me about the book you're holding in your hands, I had no idea what he was up to just yet. He asked, "Do you like witches?" Of course, I was feeling full of myself and told him no. That was a fun few minutes. I only thought I had one over on him until he asked me to write the foreword. I did two things before almost immediately agreeing: I gasped and tried not to faint. But that's Steve – he seems to always have something unexpected and exciting in the pipeline.

"No" wasn't really an untruth. I more than like witches. I fell in love with them at an incredibly young age. One of my earliest memories is of a witch. When you're only three or four years old, it's hard to separate fantasy from reality. Those wavy moments of early childhood when you're able to develop your first memories, they feel sort of dreamlike. That's when I saw The Hairy Woman. Little did I know, the creepy, wig-like hair that grew before my eyes inside an old junked car, belonged to none other than a witch—The Hairy Woman, as she was known by locals. Of course, that wasn't the last I'd see of The Hairy Woman. The lanky, long-haired witch I saw hanging back in the shadows under the well-worn underspace of huge rock would forever change me and instill a love that would grow. It was a love I would learn more about in only a few short years.

Witches have always called to me. I've never been afraid of them after the initial Hairy Woman incident, the edge of fear dulled by a thirst for knowledge.

It's not only old crones with warts holding glittering red apples in a withered hand, beckoning to alabaster-skinned young women. It's not entire houses – made of gingerbread or not - falling from the sky, leaving only a pair of shriveled legs punctuated with shiny, red shoes. It's more than a group of shrouded figures holding hands on the beach, encircling a campfire, speaking in an ages-old language or a cackling silhouette in a pointed hat riding a straw broom across the projection of a full moon. Perhaps there's more to it than green skin, warts, and a pointed hat?

As the flames begin to hungrily lick at the logs in the fire pit, the cauldron begins to boil. More fresh herbs are tossed into the concoction as the candles sputter and then blaze higher, higher still, in the background. A black cat hisses from under the table, the feather of a crow wafts slowly from the sky.

Come in and get comfortable, my friends.

Here you will learn who walks amongst us.

Here you will learn...Of Witches.

Miranda Crites
  July 30, 2020

## IN WAVES

*I*t washes over them, the water.

*He wades in, seeing her disappear again and again, the waves rising and falling on the shoreline.*

*He finds her, grabs her, pulls her close.*

*Her dress is sucked tight to her figure, he can feel the warmth of her body coming through even though the water is freezing cold.*

*Her lips find his, he doesn't protest.*

*They fall together, in waves.*

---

"Dad?"

His sons voice brings him back, steals the rest of the memory. He feels real life again, the sand, the sun, the water flowing in and out around where he sits.

"Yeah, bud?"

"Do we have to sit here?"

STEVE STRED

"Just a few more minutes, OK?"

He nods, his boy.

"You run and play, I'll stay. Sound good?"

A smile flashes as he stands and runs down the empty beach, his laughter carries over the sound of the ocean arriving on land.

He looks back over the blue, fades back to all those years ago.

---

*"WILL I SEE YOU AGAIN?"*

*"I don't know," she replies, fingers intertwining with his. She rubs the ends of his blunted nails, feels the callouses and the thickened skin.*

*"Would you want to see me again?" she finally says, her dark eyes meeting his.*

*"Absolutely," he says, pulling her closer. They sit, watching the sea froth before them, the storm finally arriving.*

---

"DAD?"

He turns, seeing his boy standing there but found he didn't recognize him with the sun hitting his eyes just so, shielded by the boy. Half of his face swollen and puffy, barnacles attached to form a cluster of holes. His left eye shut, the eyebrow hanging low from the weight of a wiggling tentacle.

"Dad, you alright?"

He blinked and there he stood, his son, returned to normal.

"Sorry, son. Lost in thought. What's up?"

"Can we go?"

"Alright."

After they loaded in the car and did a circle in the parking lot, he looked over the water once more.

---

*THERE SHE WAS, her belly prominent, wading out of the water.*

*He knew.*

*It was his.*

*She'd returned, carrying their child this time.*

*"My love," she called, before clutching her belly, face contorted in pain.*

*The boy arrived shortly, in waves.*

---

"LET'S GO, SON."

"Do we have to go to the beach again today? It's my birthday."

"Absolutely. It's a special day."

---

*"ONE DAY, I'll return. Until then, take care of our boy."*

*She left the crying child in his arms, walking away, disappearing into the water.*

---

"Dad?"

"Yeah, son?"

"Do we have to sit here?"

"Just a few more minutes, OK?"

The sun dipped low over the empty beach. The man and boy sitting side by side.

A disturbance twenty meters offshore caught his attention, transformed his face into a smile.

"Look, son. Here she comes."

She appeared from the depths, water cascading from her form as she emerged. She'd not aged a day, her hair shining as he remembered.

"Mom," his son said, standing beside him.

"Son," she called back, arms wide and inviting.

His boy changed as he ran, his bare feet kicking up wet sand with each foot fall. The barnacles returned, as did the tentacle covering his eye.

She wrapped her arms around him when he arrived, hugging him as tightly as she could. All three had tears in their eyes at the reunion. She picked him up, twirling in a circle, never once letting her feet leave the water.

"Thank you," she said, "for raising our boy."

"You're welcome," he replied.

The boy returned to him, giving him one last hug.

For now.

"I'll see you soon," he said to his son, ruffling the boy's hair. "Love you."

"Love you," he said, taking his moms hand.

He returned to the spot, *his spot*, and watched as the two made their way into deeper water.

He'd been there, every night, for the last decade, waiting for her return.

Now, as they gave one last wave and disappeared into the water, he knew he'd be coming here every night, for the next decade.

He'd sit and patiently wait for his boy to return.

———

*"WE CAN'T BE TOGETHER PHYSICALLY," she'd said, "but the water will always connect us."*

*"I know, my love," he replied.*

*The sea rolled over them, splashing where they sat, the force just enough to move them, in waves.*

### END.

IN WAVES - ABOUT

**In Waves – About**

'In Waves' came about when my son and I were playing on the beach.

I was already mentally running through story ideas for this collection and the story kind of arrived. About a man and his son, waiting for the return of the watery witch. Does it qualify as a siren? Maybe? I just wanted to create or carve out my own weird love story and the devotion that went behind that connection.

I wrote the entire first draft of this story on my phone. A bunch of the stories in this collection were done this way, which is something in the past I'd struggled attempting.

2

—————

## A CAVE, IN THE WOODS

"Ah, so you decided to come back?"

"We did."

"Finish your story, old man," Mark said, joining his sister.

"Very well. Where were we?"

"You told us about your brother going missing and your cat being found," Mark reminded him.

"That so?"

The old man took a long drink of his beer. Setting it back on the bar table, foam on his upper lip clung to the hair there.

He made an attempt to wipe it away, but he was distracted by the argument that was starting to escalate at the bar, missing most of what was on his face.

"Well, as I said, I was fifteen. My younger brother never made it home. Supposed to walk straight home from the neighbors next door. 'Straight home,' mom had said. When night fell and the police arrived, I figured he was dead and gone."

"So, how does the cat come into play?"

"The cat?"

"The cat."

Mark stared at the old man. He wanted to storm out, leave this hole-in-the-wall bar behind, but they'd put out a call for their podcast, and a listener had told them that an old drunk – in this *very* bar – had a story that would scare them to their core.

So, he stayed.

"Oh, yes. The cat. Well, a few days go by, search groups still out, posters on the power poles and such, as they used to do before your digital world took over. Simpler days. Anyways, I went to the back yard, wanting some time to think. I found our cat."

"What was with the cat?"

Megan was taking notes, which had pissed her off to no end. The man had steadfastly refused to be recorded, said that the device would fry his voice, that what was on the gizmo wouldn't be what he said. 'Incorrect words' had been his exact quote.

"The cat came back. Didn't know he was a gonner. But that cat had come back, and he shouldn't've run away."

Mark laughed. He should've stifled it, kept it buried, but it burst out before he could stop himself.

"Shut. The. Fuck. Up."

The four words spoken forcefully by the old man erased all humor. Mark mimed that he was zipping his lips and tossing the key away.

"You think my brother going missing and my cat being beheaded is funny, you cocksucker? You think that's funny, boy? Do ya? Do ya?"

Bar goers turned now, watching the old man get worked up, his voice growing louder and louder.

"No, no. Sorry. Fuck, sorry. I didn't know."

The old man took another drink, glaring at Mark.

"Look, Mr… sir, we're sorry. My brother's sorry. Please, go on," Megan said, placing a comforting hand on the old mans.

"Well, there was my cat. Head sitting beside the body. Wasn't a clean cut. Looked hacked. Sticky. And a note. Scrawled letters in charcoal. I'll never forget those words," he said, taking another drink. He clanked the empty mug on the tabletop, the bartender rushing to refill.

"What did it say?" Megan asked.

"In a cave. In the woods."

"That's what was written on the note?"

"Do I look like a liar?"

The glare returned, levelled on Megan this time.

"I can still feel the depression of the letters under my fingertips. I can."

He absently ran his hand back and forth over the sticky tabletop surface.

"So, what did you do?"

"I went."

"You went?"

"I went. Alone."

"Alone?"

"Alone."

"What did you find?"

Megan looked to Mark; her eyes blazed like they always did when she found an opening she wanted to exploit for the listeners.

"At first, nothing. I didn't tell no one, not even my mom. I just rushed off into the woods, running as fast as I could."

He stopped, taking another long drink. Mark joined him, downing some of his own suds, but Megan was locked onto the man's face, practically begging for him to go on.

"I was lost. I knew it. So, I decided... I decided I'd turn around and go home. A failure. My brother was out there and I wasn't going to find him. So, I turned and started walking back, knowing that I would need to tell my mom."

Another drink.

"Then, I heard the voice."

"The voice?"

"The voice."

"Was it your brother? What was your brother's name?"

"It was a woman's voice. And I ain't said it yet."

Another glare.

From behind them, someone changed the song on the old jukebox that still lived in the corner of the dance floor. Mark grimaced at the 80's rock. A woman screamed and a man whooped, the party just starting for that group.

It was the man whooping that got the drunk speaking again.

"The woman called for me. Knew my name and

everything. She said '*Henry, come my boy. Come, your brother is here.*' Then she was singing, but not with words."

"Not with words?"

"Not with words."

"Humming?"

"Sure, humming. Only not."

Megan let out a huff, annoyed with the man's evasiveness.

"I started after that tune, not running, but not leisurely walking either. I knew something wasn't right, but my *brother*... was out there."

"What happened next?" Megan asked, scribbling as fast as she could.

"The woods changed. I didn't immediately notice it. Little differences flickered in the periphery of my eyes as I searched for the source of the singing. She had to be ahead of me?"

The man's eyes glossed over, Mark watching as he was reliving those moments. The eyes darted, looking everywhere and nowhere all at once.

"There he was," he started, before sputtering to a stop, followed by crying. Mark and Megan looked at each other, unsure what to do. They'd never had an elderly drunk burst into sobs in front of them before.

Megan scooted around to sit beside the man, placing her arms around his shoulders, comforting.

She rubbed his back until he sniffed in deeply.

"Sorry about that. All these years later, still hurts, you know?"

Megan gave him a genuine smile, Mark saw, surprised with her caring.

She moved back over, picking up the pen.

"Carry on, when ready, sir," she said.

"Name's Eric," he said, taking a drink. Mark and Megan looked at each other. That wasn't right. They both knew that. He'd said earlier his name was Henry. *Glug, glug,* Megan mouthed, pretending to take a drink. Mark shrugged.

"Ok, where was I? Ah, yes. There he was. He matched the cat you see. He was off the ground, poor... poor... Henry. Six feet for sure. Hands and legs tied and pulled wide, hanging over the ground from two trees. His head... it sat on a rock in front of the body... and as though Henry sensed I'd arrived; the head swivelled all the way around so that it was looking at me, he was looking at me."

The man stopped, looking close to vomiting. He took another drink, eyes never meeting Megan or Mark's.

"So, the head turned around and looked at you?"

"Yes."

"What happened next?" Mark said, realizing he sounded impatient. "I'm sorry. Take your time. This story is just so amazing."

"It ain't no goddamned story. It's my life."

Mark thought for sure, this time, the man would stand and leave, but he remained seated across from them.

"What happened next still keeps me awake. It's why I drink."

As if to make a point of the impact, he took another long swig, finishing the mug. He clanked it against the bar, a new drink appearing before him in a flash.

"My brother's body began to convulse and shake, as

though it was being electrocuted. I couldn't take my eyes from it, but for some reason my attention returned to my brother's head. His mouth opened; I could see something struggling to come out of it, but I couldn't understand from where? You see... he had no neck. I gagged when a python's head poked free, its tongue darting in and out. From where had it came? Who knows? But I stood and watched in horror as twenty feet of snake slithered from my brother's decapitated head. All the while his body shook and strained to break the confines that had it strung up in the trees in the first place."

Megan was writing as fast as she could. Mark sat, staring at the man, trying to process what he was saying. Surely, this was a big put on? The man playing them for a fool.

"At the end, when the snake's tail exited his mouth, I thought at first his tongue had stuck to the tip, being pulled out behind. But I soon saw, it was his innards. His guts and his intestines came through, somehow being pulled out of his body... a body that hung from trees a dozen feet behind!"

He slammed his mug to the tabletop, beer splashing out of the glass and sloshing around it. Megan tried to calm the man, the patrons of the bar that were near glanced over, wondering what was happening.

Mark knew it now. He knew this drunk was a fraud, paid to tell them a ridiculous story.

"Alright, you got us. Sure, sure. Big scary story," Mark began. "What happened next? Bigfoot arrive?" He let out a snort, smirk plastered on his face.

The man leveled a look on Mark that he'd never seen

before. A scowl that made his testicles tuck up between his ass cheeks.

"You little fucking punk. You come in here, asking questions about my past and then decide to antagonize me? *Me*? Fuck you. Go. I'm done."

The color drained from Mark's face. Megan glared at Mark, pissed that he'd ruined their segment. The man took a sip of his foam-topped beer, eyes not leaving Mark's.

"I'm sorry. I really am. Please, go on," Mark said, bordering on pleading.

"$100."

"$100?"

"$100."

Mark looked from the old man to Megan. She nodded.

He pulled out his wallet, grabbing two fifties and sliding them to the man. When the man reached out to the grab them, Mark didn't move his hand.

"But you finish this story. I'll keep my trap shut, but you finish."

"I'll finish."

The old man took his time while he composed himself. He nodded, letting Megan know he was ready to continue.

"So. Like I said, everything flew out of Eric's mouth and once this python dragging his insides had disappeared into the forest, I looked at the body still hanging, but now it's deflated. Looks like when someone's lost three hundred pounds, you know. All saggy and wrinkly. From the darkness behind, I heard something. A crack of a stick. I don't remember exactly, just something made a noise and I looked. Behind the trees, set back in the shadows was the opening of a cave. It was triangular, the entrance and I could see the silhouette of someone standing there, watching me."

"What happened next?" Megan asked. Mark could see that she believed every word coming from his mouth. He still thought it was a scam, and not because he was out $100. And while he was pissed, he knew they could turn this into a stunning segment on the podcast. Maybe even an entire episode.

"Well, she spoke to me. This old wretched, hag sang my name. She never stepped into the light. Nope, not a once. I could see her long fingernails and crusted hair, matted with dirt. But she stayed just back there, out of sight. Then she started humming. I couldn't believe it. I raised off the ground, floating towards her, knowing I'd never be found."

"How did you get away?" Mark asked.

"Who said I did?"

The man's eyes flashed and shimmered, the lights in the room flickering before going dark.

Mark and Megan heard a noise that sounded like nails on a chalkboard before both felt nothing.

---

MARK WAS the first to wake.

He screamed a guttural scream when he saw he was looking at his body before him, strung up between two trees.

"Who said I did?" the voice said, followed by laughter. The silhouette from the cave, in the woods shifted, getting Mark's attention.

A scream nearby came from Megan. Mark knew her head was sitting feet from him. Her body would be in the trees as well.

He could feel the wiggling of something from deep in his throat, which made him gag. He knew what was to come. The python would slither out, pulling his insides with it.

From the darkened entrance the hag cackled, licking her cracked lips.

Even from here, Mark could smell beer.

### END.

# A CAVE, IN THE WOODS - ABOUT

Seems a fairly straight ahead story, yeah?

Haha!

Story #2 in the collection and this one is once again, somehow inspired by my son. He has such a vivid imagination already and when we play with his toys, he'll come up with these elaborate places..

Well, recently he decided that Godzilla was going to sleep in a cave. In the woods.

Much like when we stumbled on the idea for 'The Window In the Ground,' the idea blasted into my head and I rumbled through it.

One thing I'll add – much like my story 'James' in 'Left Hand Path: 13 more tales of black magick' I decided to entertain the idea of the serpent within. I personally don't see enough of the serpent reflections in occult/witch stories, but when you read about it online, snakes are often very important figures in the myths around them.

# 3

## GRANDMA'S LETTERS

She died alone and lonely.

His grandma. His Nan.

He should've gone to see her, visit her one time in the hospital.

But things happened.

"*Life,*" he'd say to anyone who cared or listened.

Truthfully, he was lazy. He was scared. Who wanted to see their loved one in the hospital? Laying in that bed, machines beeping. Would she even be awake? If she was sleeping, what did it matter if he visited or not? Not like she'd know he was there. Sure, the nurses would say, "*your grandson, Tommy came by. What a nice guy, he sat in your room for twenty minutes.*" Nah, wasn't for him.

Imagine his surprise, when the letter arrived. Her estate. The house was his.

She didn't have any money. Figures. Never his luck.

Even worse, he can't afford to keep the place. He'll need to go, clean it out and sell it.

*What a hassle*, he thinks.

He doesn't even want to think how long it'll take him to go through her stuff. He figures she was most likely a hoarder. Weren't most old people? He'll find a bunch of junk, which will cost him money to throw out and then he'll have to deal with some suit that'll want a percentage to sell the house.

On the drive to her place, he wonders if her TV has an HDMI port, eyeing his PS3 sitting on the passenger seat. He didn't want to forfeit much screen time with this ridiculous task. This was one of the few times he wished his parents were still around. They'd been great when he was a kid, but as soon as he graduated all they cared about was his moving out and getting a job.

The driveway is a single car cement pad. No garage. The house, one level. He remembers all the times they came here over the years. The old furniture, the hard, sucking candy in the dish. He expects to have nostalgia wash over him when he slips the key in the lock and opens the door.

Smells, photos, memories.

Instead he finds a completely bare house.

He enters the small foyer. From there he passes the mirrored closet where he always hung his jacket, into the living room. No couch, no chair. No coffee table. No entertainment unit or TV. Nothing.

Down the short hall, each of the two bedrooms are stripped clean. As is the bathroom.

He doesn't find anything until he enters the kitchen.

The table is gone. As is the stove, fridge and dishwasher. The only thing he spots is a brown box sitting by the sink.

A note is taped to the top, where the panels have been tucked into each other to keep it closed.

He snaps it off, part of the paper left behind with the tape.

He gives it a cursory read, before feeling rage. Leaning against the counter he rereads it.

*Tommy.*

*I wrote this when the doctor's told me I wasn't going home.*

*You're a piece of shit human. It hurts me to think that, let alone write that about my own grandson. I would've said this to you in person, but I knew you'd never come to the hospital. The house looks weird all empty doesn't it? I had my lawyer arrange to sell off all my possessions. I didn't want your grubby hands on any of the money that would come from a sale. The only thing I had him leave was the box this was taped on.*

*Inside, you'll find letters. It's up to you what you do with them. You can toss this entire box in the garbage, angry that someone had the nerve to say something so true about you, or you can read through them and see what's in them.*

*The choice is yours.*

*Also, the house has already sold. I know you thought you were going to need to sell it, but this was the only way I could think of, to get you here again and to read this letter. You'll not get any money from me.*

*Grandma*

*PS – in order to ensure you don't have a tantrum and break everything in here, the police will be arriving shortly. When you unlocked the door, it notified my lawyer and he's put in a call to police. Best get on your way.*

. . .

TOMMY WAS LIVID. He grabbed the box and stormed out, not even taking the time to close the door to the house.

The entire drive home was done in a rage. He was seething. He wanted to toss that box out of the car window and watch it disappear in the rear-view mirror. But something kept him from doing that. The lure of the unknown.

By the time he arrived at his apartment complex, he was determined to go through each and every letter and teach his grandma a lesson. No matter what she thought of him, he wasn't going to quit on this task. He parked in his assigned spot, plopped his PS3 and controller on the box and made his way to the elevator.

While going up to the fourth floor, he noticed a musky odor emanating from the box. It was off-putting. As though the box had been wet before and left to dry.

When he entered his apartment, his roommate was talking on his headset to someone, while playing a videogame. Normally, Tommy would sit down and watch, but not today. He wanted to figure this out ASAP and be done with it.

He closed the door to his room, setting his PS3 on the floor by his TV. Dumping the letters to the floor, he saw there was a significant number of them. As he began looking through them, he saw it was all the same.

Each piece of paper, in each envelope had one letter of the alphabet on it and a number. As he shuffled through the papers, growing more frustrated, he realized that he needed to lay them out in order to see what they spelled.

He went and grabbed a Coke, sipping from the can while he watched his roommate make some progress in his game. Once done, he returned to his room, anger rising to a boiling point again, seeing the papers all strewn about.

"Fuck it," he said to the room. He proceeded to arrange them in numerical order. Hours later, he'd moved clothes, his mattress and even shifted his dresser, just so that the loose pages of paper, each featuring one infuriating letter on it, were in order.

Impulsively he wanted to read it, see what this final note from his inconsiderate grandma said, but he also wanted to be the one in charge of what was happening. So, he left the room, grabbed another Coke and plopped down in the gaming chair beside his roommate.

"You get any money," Jason asked, staying focused on the game.

"Nope. The bitch made a point of not leaving me anything."

"Dude, that's your grandma."

"*Was.*"

He left Jason playing his game, annoyed at what he'd said, returning to his room.

He stood, staring at the pages on the floor of his room.

*Now or never.*

It was either time to read the message or just burn all the pages.

. . .

*TOMMY.*

*This is the real letter I wanted to leave for you, but not in public view for any prying eyes. You see, the house and the stuff that filled it were meaningless to me. While you may question that and think about the monetary value, for me that meant nothing. It was the location of the house. The drawing of the energy, the axis to nature's powers.*

*I am what many call a witch.*

*You may scoff or snicker at that, but I guarantee you, by the end of this letter you'll believe.*

*I'm sorry you turned into such a waste of space. Your mother and father were beside themselves that you were so lazy. Had no drive, no desire.*

*What does that have to do with this letter?*

*We believe in harnessing power, or the ability to control and manipulate things to do our bidding. So, Tommy, I'm going to use you to do what I need. You're probably thinking no chance.*

*But so far, you've done everything I've asked. Went to the house, retrieved the box, assembled the message and you are now reading it.*

*Total control.*

*Which brings us to the end. But also, a beginning. Or more accurately, a restart.*

*This was all a test. For me to see just how powerful my abilities have become.*

*You unfortunately will be the sacrifice.*

*Tommy, you've played your part.*

*If what I've casted is correct, you'll go to sleep for the last time, as I return to the world of the living.*

. . .

TOMMY FOUND he was close to laughter when he finished. His grandma had obviously suffered from dementia at the end of her life, losing her grip on reality.

He kicked the ordered pages with anger, before scooping them up and tossing them into the garbage.

Grabbing his third Coke, he rejoined Jason, fuming over his grandma playing him for a fool.

A part of him, though, couldn't stop glancing back at those papers.

Every few minutes, Tommy would side-eye them, expecting a few pages to have fallen from the bin and landed on the floor.

Hour after hour this went on, even while he paid for pizza they'd ordered, too lazy to make even KD, Tommy glanced at the bin, not noticing that he gave the pizza guy an extra $20 by mistake.

"Dude?"

Tommy looked over at Jason, not realizing he'd been transfixed for some time on the trash.

"Dude, I asked, can I have the last slice?"

"Yeah, yeah," Tommy replied, giving a half-hearted wave.

"Man, you're out of it. Go get some sleep."

At Jason's mention of sleep, Tommy felt a cold chill roll over him.

He knew he had to sleep eventually, but why was he now dreading it? He didn't actually believe that his grandma was capable of returning from the dead, did he? *Wouldn't that make her a zombie, not a witch*, he thought, bringing a smile to his face.

"K. I'm off to bed. I get to *actually* have a turn tomorrow," he joked as he went to his room, leaving Jason in front of the TV.

When he stepped in, everything was *off.*

The air was thick and smelled like dirt.

He noticed his Batman wall clock had frozen in time, the hands ticking but no motion happening. Tommy was genuinely freaked out.

"It's just my brain. Just my brain over thinking everything. Just my brain," he said, sliding into bed. He made sure to tuck the blankets over his feet and pulled them far from the edge of the bed.

While Tommy was scared, he was also very tired, drifting off to sleep in no time at all.

---

A COLD BREEZE and the feeling of someone stroking his cheek caused his eyes to snap open.

She sat beside him in bed, crooked teeth showing from between her cracked smile.

Tommy wanted to sit but found his body wouldn't respond. He looked at his grandma, her face distorted and mashed, as though a cheap movie mask was being worn.

"Grandma?"

"Shhh," she said, putting a finger to his lips. "Thank you for bringing me back."

She leaned close and began to blow into his ear as though she was attempting to snuff out birthday candles on a cake.

At first all Tommy felt was her breath, but slowly his body began to tingle.

He was able to look down over his nose just enough to see that his blanket had been pulled back. As he watched, the tingling he was experiencing was his body transforming into dust.

"Grandma, please?" he begged.

"My boy, not this time. Not this time."

The breeze picked up again and he cried as his body was blown away. Section by section his remains were lifted and sparkled as the air caught hold and carried it through the open window.

Everything grew blurry and fuzzy.

The tingling made its way up his chest and neck and when it finally arrived at his head, he wasn't even able to shed a tear.

END.

# GRANDMA'S LETTERS - ABOUT

'Grandma's Letters' came from the same place my story 'Wardrobe Malfunction' came from. We never truly know the 'real' person. We think we know someone but even then we don't know everything. We see it on the news all the time "he was a nice guy, never suspected he'd do that," or "she seemed like such a nice woman, can't believe this happened." For many people, something lurks just below the surface and it usually never comes above water.

In this case, our ungrateful, ass-hat of a grandson learns a lesson the hard way.

* 'Wardrobe Malfunction' is published in my collection 'Left Hand Path: 13 more tales of black magick.'

## 4

## THREE WORDS

S o it was, on the second day of camping, I left our tent to take a piss. I shuffled off in the morning dew, socks getting wet but my bladder bursting full.

As I lowered the front of my boxer shorts and felt the stream begin to flow, I glanced into the trees and made eye contact with the crone.

My heart thudded with an intensity I didn't know existed before, my bladder continuing to drain.

She let a sly grin creep across her lips, her darkened eyes never moving from mine.

Something cracked in the woods off to my side, my eyes darted for the briefest of moments, but upon returning to the woman, I found the space now deserted.

"Honey?"

I hadn't even heard Kim exit the tent, but when I looked back, she was standing there staring at me. Arms crossed, covering her bare breasts. Normally the sight of her standing in the woods wearing only a thong would've got me worked up and I would've chased her around camp, laughing and squealing until we went back in the tent to fuck.

Not this morning.

"Are you OK, Trent?" she asked.

"Ah... sure... sorry, still foggy from last night," I managed, returning to her side.

Before following her back in the tent, I looked once again to that spot, but no hag stared back.

———

WE PACKED IN SILENCE.

Well, my silence.

Kim was blabbing on about her RRSP work and how another day hiking was going to be so rewarding for our souls.

I was lost in thought. Speculation, really.

At what had been watching me.

———

THE SMELL of beans being cooked in a can had always made me smile.

It was my lack of enthusiasm for lunch that got Kim's attention and she once again asked if I was doing alright.

"Just tired," I replied, which did the trick. We still had two more hours of walking before us, which brought me down even more thinking about it.

We ate while making small talk, the shorter my replies

the more frustrated Kim became and all at once I realized she was starting to head out.

"Hey, wait up," I shouted, watching her stop on the path ahead.

"Trent, I told you twenty minutes ago to get moving and you remained sitting there. I'm not waiting any longer."

She turned and kept walking, leaving me alone.

Once I lost sight of her, I immediately felt eyes on me from behind. I refused to turn. Instead, I slung my pack over my shoulders, rushing to catch up to Kim, ignoring the rough breathing that followed.

———

It took me fifteen minutes of walking as fast as I could, to the point of nearly jogging, that I finally caught up to Kim. She gave me an annoyed look, as though a part of her had hoped I had decided to turn and walk the other direction.

"Hey," I said, trying to sound friendly.

"Yup," was her curt reply.

We stared for a minute, neither speaking. After realizing we were at a standstill, Kim was fed up. She began to walk away when she froze, staring straight ahead. I took a step before seeing she'd stopped and when I looked beyond her, I saw why.

There she was.

The crone.

Her right arm was raised, extended forward, her pencil thin, index finger pointed at the two of us.

We stood in silence waiting for the end. A proclamation or some yelled words that would cause the world to engulf us.

Instead, her cracked, dirt covered lips opened ever so slightly and she whispered three words.

Neither myself nor Kim heard them, just the cadence and rise and fall of the three.

I struggled to keep my stomach contents down, my eyes having discerned the rotting teeth behind those lips. Even from this distance, a stench assaulted our noses, partly from her body, partly from speaking.

I was in a daze, my mind rapidly trying to formulate what those three words had been.

I didn't notice that Kim had taken a step towards her, or that my girlfriend's posture had changed from laid back to confrontational.

"Who the fuck are you? Some old, lost crackhead? You need us to call an ambulance?"

My head snapped up, hearing Kim's tone. Filled with disgust and judgement.

The woman's tattered rags that adorned her skeletal frame, fluttered around her as she herself took a step towards Kim. The movement disarmed my normally unintimidated girlfriend, and Kim shrunk as she stepped back herself.

"You speak so flippantly for someone already dead."

Kim's mouth fell open and I found I was shaking with equal parts fear and equal parts anger. Before we could say a word, the hag turned and stepped behind a tree. I rushed forward, but much to my surprise found no trace of her, as though she'd disappeared into thin air.

"Wow. She was nuts, wasn't she? And so far out here. Must be a homeless camp nearby."

Kim started hiking again, as though nothing had happened. I wanted to tell her just how absurd her statement had been. A homeless camp? Three days hike into the woods? No chance. Instead, I kept my mouth shut and followed, still trying to figure out what had been whispered.

---

Two HOURS later arrived we at a spot Kim said was perfect for the night. We set up our tent, thoughts of the hag long since having left my head.

I got a fire going in no time, while Kim got the tent set up, air mattress inflated, and dinner prepped.

I wanted to make a comment about how my task was infinitely harder than hers, but she was a far superior camper than I, so I didn't say anything, as I knew she'd have a quick comeback.

Instead, I took a seat on the ground by the fire, poked at it with a stick I'd found and waited to start cooking food.

And waited.

And waited.

And then it dawned on me that Kim wasn't at the tent or near the fire. I looked around frantically, wondering if she'd said something again that I'd missed.

"Kim?"

I circled the tent, circled the area.

"Kim?" I called louder.

I froze. There was a sound.

I stayed still, waiting to hear if it came again.

A soft, subtle crinkle of leaves being broken caught my ear.

It was straight ahead, in the trees before me. I took a few tentative steps towards the sound, feeling my heart pound against my chest.

"Kim?"

"Nuggghhhh..."

I darted forward at the noise, pushing through the thick bushes that bordered the trees and acted as a perimeter around where we'd set up camp. Once I made it through, I spotted a shape and froze.

It was Kim.

Sort of.

She was writhing and convulsing on the forest floor, her body spasming as she let out pained "nuhhgggssss" and "eeeerrrrrsss," sounds. I wanted to grab her and hold her down, help her in some way, but as she twisted again and her face was in full view, I knew not to move any closer.

Half of her face was Kim, the other half was the crone. As her features changed and transformed, her bones broke and reformed, taking on the shape of the woman who'd appeared before us.

Kim's cracked lips moved in a repeated pattern I soon realized. Her lips opened and closed, opened and closed, and my emotions could no longer be contained as I now knew what those three words had been, that the crone had whispered while pointing.

Kim was now forming the words, but not speaking

them, preventing the curse put on her from being passed to me.

As the transformation completed and the last vestiges of my love, left this mortal plain, I turned and ran.

I left the tent and our belongings behind, running as fast as I could down the trail, knowing I had three days of running before I'd even get to my truck.

Behind me, I could hear the echoes of the hag laughing at my cowardness.

I didn't care. Those three words would haunt me for the rest of my days.

"Now, I'm you," she'd whispered.

"Now, I'm you."

END

# THREE WORDS - ABOUT

Another story written entirely on my phone, 'Three Words' came about from my research into my story 'The Witch' which was previously released in my collection 'Left Hand Path: 13 more tales of black magick,' and reappears next in this very collection.

While researching 'The Witch' one thing I continued to note in old witch trial stories and write-ups, was that very frequently "testimony" (and take that with a grain of salt) would suggest that those accused of being a witch would whisper a curse at the afflicted.

That idea has stuck in my head for about four years now. I even had a word doc in my idea folder that simply said "witch whispering." So, when the ideas began to roll in for this collection, I knew I would be finally writing a story with that idea as the back bone.

## 5

## THE WITCH

ORIGINALLY PUBLISHED IN LEFT HAND
PATH: 13 MORE TALES OF BLACK MAGICK

T he candles lit the small hut, the wind gusted, the sound echoing off the wooden planks which made up the outside walls. The old woman, pushing her thinning grey hair from her face, shuffled over to her table, thick skirt flowing around her legs, ingredients laid out.

The skin on her face was cracked with a thousand age lines, her nose long, mouth scowling. It had been a month since she had watched her sister burn at the stake, hidden away from prying eyes, staying at the back of the crowd, her screams of pain travelling through the air with ease as the flames grew higher and higher. The villagers stoked the fire long into the night, long after her sister had ceased to live.

She shuffled to the table and inspected her ingredients, anger and vengeance flowing through her mind and her veins. Her sister may have been stupid, may have been exposed, but she wouldn't be forgotten. The town folk responsible for her death would be dealt with one-by-one, and in short order.

She flipped open her old leather notebook, carefully going through the fragile pages, before finally coming to the cast she wanted. Her sneer turned into a grin.

"Yes, yes, this will do just fine," she said out loud, to no one in particular. Gathering the ingredients she went over to the fire, tossing them in, one at a time, while yelling out the cast in an ancient language.

Outside the trees shuddered and the animals cringed, the earth having not heard this tongue for centuries.

---

FOR DECADES the villagers had suspected witchcraft to be permeating their pleasant existence. Every so often the weather would change, the crops would suffer, and some small animals or a young child would mysteriously disappear.

The village elders noticed a trend. Whenever something would occur, it wasn't long after a complaint was made concerning the family that lived on the outskirts of town. Three small huts, made of wood, set back into a bank, tree roots anchoring the structures to the ground.

*"What can we do?"* Would more often than not be the sentiment towards the three small huts. Plans would be hatched and plots would be plotted, but as they technically didn't live in the township, people were wary about their own punishment, should they take justice into their own hands.

One such man attempted to extract his own justice. Colonel Frank Douglas III, a former Army man, who after his three year old son went missing, grabbed his rifle and hiked out to question the tenants of the huts. The last time anyone saw Colonel Douglas III was as he left the village, rifle in hand, anger in his steps. His son's body was found a few days later. It was placed, along with Colonel Douglas III's war medals, near the last spot Colonel Douglas III had been seen alive, a small wood marker noting the location.

Then there had been nothing for some time, the villagers mistakenly believing that the owners of the three small huts had passed away, and age finally serving the justice they longed to have. But they were wrong.

The three dwellings belonged to the three sisters. They were born and raised in the huts and grew up loathing the villagers. Shunned by society, the parents of the sisters grew jaded towards the outside world, becoming more and more withdrawn. The outward appearances showed this, the yards not maintained, windows covered in filth.

But the sisters didn't mind. This was home, and inside they were ravenous students. As the years went by, and their parents grew sicker, they went further into the dark arts, down the pathway laid before them by their parents and their grandparents before them.

They continued to curse the town, ensuring droughts would occur, food production halted and every so often, an animal or child would be picked off.

The oldest sister Rebecca, became the most reclusive of the group, barricading herself, not venturing out for years at a time. The middle sister Rachel, grew such hatred to the town that she was constantly plotting and scheming of ways to inflict pain and hurt on the towns-folk. The youngest of the three was different. Sarah sought out social interaction. She would often disguise herself, change her appearance, and walk into town. She would attend fairs, carnivals and parades, basking in the joy the other people had, wishing that she could share this with her family.

It was on one of these trips that Sarah entered a tavern, hearing the saddened warble of the lone bard on the stage, no crowd before him.

*"I sing my sad song, for those who would hear,*
*But nary an eye and nary an ear,*
*Listen to my tune of lonely lament,*
*For my body will be found by the riverbank."*

Sarah felt the pain in each word, causing her to exhale sharply.

The bard heard the sound and stopped playing, laying his instrument down. He left the stage and approached, surprised to have an audience.

"I am sorry, my fair lady, I had not known you had entered. For if I had, I would have played something happier, not something that talks about my own ending."

"My dear bard, your song was beautiful. It touched my soul, and spoke to me like nothing has before. I fear loneliness is my curse in life and will not have the love of any others."

The bard couldn't believe he had found such a kindred soul, and thus the courtship began. Every day, Sarah would head into town, meeting with the bard, and listening to him perform. Then the two would dash off, young lovers enjoying their time together. They would walk through the parks, hand in hand, feeling the sun shine on their faces, even when the sky was covered in clouds.

Soon though, the bard began to suspect something was foul with his new love. Sometimes, when he looked at her beautiful face, at the right angle, he would see an old woman, weathered and worn, staring back at him. Other times, he would notice that she was walking with a limp, or a strange odor would permeate the air around them, of mould and rot, making him feel ill to his stomach.

He wasn't the only one to suspect something was up.

Rachel too, began to grow suspicious. She knew her youngest sister liked to visit the town, and as much as she detested the entire lot of them, she didn't mind, as long as the disguises changed and no suspicion was brought towards them.

So it was, during the third month of the courtship, that Rachel realized that for each day Sarah went into town, her disguise wasn't changing. It was the same, day in and day out, and so Rachel followed the youngest as she went into town.

She watched as her sister went into the tavern, lurked as she watched Sarah swaying rhythmically to the sounds of the bard, and stalked them as the two walked hand in hand, through the park. It took everything within her to not strike them both dead, when she viewed Sarah use an incantation to shine some sun down on the two, as the rain fell all around.

She was disgusted by this display and turned away,

heading back to the huts. She waited, until she heard her youngest sibling return home, before heading over to confront her.

Barging in, she was just in time to witness the transformation back to the old lady she knew so well.

"What is the meaning of this? I witnessed you parading around with that musician. Do you not believe he will see the real you? Do you not know this charade will not end well? Has the memory of mother and father swinging by their necks from the trees faded so, that you would risk persecution? For what? Hand holding and his soft lips?"

Sarah was distressed by being discovered.

"How dare you. How dare you follow me and spy? I have the right to be happy and to enjoy life. You and that old hag next door may refuse to embrace the day, but I for one will not shun it, not one day more. I am in love, and it feels good to have those feelings reciprocated."

"This cannot occur. Does he not know? Is he not aware that you are well over five hundred years old? We live in a world of darkness, pain and evil powers. We can't simply cavort with the human existence. They do not understand us and they ensure our kind continues to be pushed down, exiled and eradicated. Mark my words sister, he will see through this cloak you have placed on yourself, and when he does your ending will be swift and painful."

With that, Rachel, slammed the wooden door behind her, returning to her hut to simmer, knowing full well that trouble would be coming their way soon.

Sarah was undaunted by her older siblings' veiled

threats. She remembered her parents. She remembered her mother smiling at her as the horse was swatted, running away, and removing the platform below her feet. She remembered the sound of her parent's necks as their body weight halted suddenly at the length of the thick rope, the sound of their necks breaking.

Their bodies were there for weeks, the crows coming by, picking bits of flesh away. The wind blew lightly, causing them to sway back and forth gently, the sound of the rope around the branch creaking and groaning. Then one day, the two of them were gone and she stopped visiting.

This wouldn't happen to her, and to confirm the love they shared, she quickly transformed and fled back to the village, to her bard, to a storm brewing before her.

Arriving at the tavern, the scene playing out before her was crushing. There was her love, her bard, serenading a young lady at the front table, eyes locked.

Her fury and wrath blinded her from the idea that this was his job, and that maybe he did in fact love her, but in order to make money, he would sing to other females.

She was having none of it, speaking a cast under her breath as she stayed on the periphery watching the tableau play out.

Screams of pain emanated from the table, and the bard jumped back in horror as the lovely young woman began to liquefy in front of him. She melted quickly, into a pool of waste at the base of the table.

The tavern was upended with terror and fear. How could this happen? What was the meaning of this? It was then the bard spotted his love in the back of the bar and he knew instantly that what he had suspected was true.

"WITCH!" He yelled, pointing his instrument at her. She turned to flee, but it was too late. She was swarmed quickly and grabbed by the mob.

Rachel was alerted to her younger sister's detaining by a grumpy old owl who came by, needing to repay its debt. She wasted no time, forgave the debt and alerted Rebecca.

"Who cares? Serves her right for being in everyone's business."

Leaving her, Rachel went into the village as fast as she could, wanting to witness as much of the trial as she could.

Under a cloak of disguise, she slipped into the back of the small courthouse just as her younger sibling was led in, shackled at wrist and ankle, burlap sack placed over her head.

The gathered crowd began to vent, hurling obscenities and a few rocks at the accused.

The gavel pounded the Magistrate's bench three times, as the old man yelled "ORDER!"

Soon the crowd went silent, and her sister's face was revealed.

The crowd let out a collective gasp, for this wasn't the young beautiful lady who had been detained in the tavern, but an ancient hag, weathered and grotesque.

Once again the Magistrate pounded his gavel, telling the attendees to bring the court to order or to leave at once.

The crowd hushed low, not wanting to leave, wanting to see this out.

"Ma'am, I am the Honourable Magistrate Hawthorne. Are you aware of the charges against you?"

"I am," Sarah replied in a shrill, cracked voice that showed her age. As she spoke the wind picked up outside and the attendees looked around, cringing slightly, hearing the building moan.

"As this is a court under God, and under his authority, what say you to these charges before us?"

"I am no Witch. You all killed my parents, but I long ago forgave you all. I was simply looking for love, and the young bard supplied it. How am I supposed to know how he views me?"

Chaos erupted again, as the gathered crowd hurled more obscenities, clearly infuriated that she denied being a Witch.

"ORDER! I will not have this language in this court, under God's watch."

"Sir, may I speak?"

A soft voice arose from the corner, and as the middle sister looked, she saw it was the bard.

"You may, but I will hold you responsible for any language unbefitting this place. Do you understand?"

"Your honour, I do. I am the bard of whom she speaks. I was in love with a lady, who brightened my day, and changed my songs from sorrow to sunshine. On the night in question, I was singing one of those very songs to Miss Abigail, on her wedding eve. When she... when she melted in front of me, I saw a demon in the corner of the tavern. I had seen the side of the demon before. I thought my eyes were playing tricks on me, but I knew, in my heart of hearts, that the lady I had fallen for was a heathen. I was so blinded by this new joy I chose to ignore it, and by doing so I put everyone in harm's way. For that I am truly sorry. To Daniel, I am so sorry for Miss Abigail passing because of my tune. But as I stand here before you, your honour, I know it was this old crow that caused the death, as true as my word is to God."

The Magistrate was nodding his head in agreement.

"There is no question to me, that you, as you sit here before us, were responsible for the death of Miss Abigail. You clearly used some blinding disguise to ensure the bard would be enraptured with you. But there is no denying the outcome. A young woman may have been detained, but the Sheriff and his men placed that lady in a guarded cell with a burlap sack over her head, and when they retrieved her this day, to bring her to court, you are what was under that sack.

Witchcraft was at play from the beginning, and because of this, and the attack on Miss Abigail, I sentence you to be burned at the stake. Punishment to be completed tomorrow as the Church bells ring noon."

With that he banged his gavel three times and the room erupted in cheers.

Rachel waited long enough to watch Sarah being led back out of the courtroom, and then swiftly returned to her hut. She knew Rebecca wouldn't care, so she didn't even make an effort to tell her what was happening.

That night she went to sleep furious. Furious that her little sister let herself get caught, and furious that she would have to protect herself and Rebecca, who wouldn't make any effort to stop the villagers.

In the morning, the light crept through the dirty windows, waking Rachel from her angered slumber. She arose, transformed, and then headed into town, prepared to watch the death of her sibling.

The burning went without a hitch.

The stake was erected, the guilty dragged out from the jail holding-cell and affixed to the wood. Below her, bushels of branches were stacked up, and finally the Sheriff walked out.

"Witch, you have been sentenced to death, for the murder of Miss Abigail. The sentence will be carried out by myself, under the orders of the Honourable Magistrate, and you shall be burned at the stake. I ask you, do you have any last words?"

Rachel, mingling in the crowd and keeping her presence as low-key as she could, craned her ears when this was asked.

From the stake, she was surprised to hear her sister speak.

"I do," she screeched, her face hideous, covered in dirt.

"I want to say thank you. Thank you to the bard, for showing me what the love of a stranger felt like. Thank you to my older sisters, for caring for me all these years, without mother and father. And to all of you gathered here, I hope the sight of my death haunts you until the end of time. May you all be cursed!"

With that, she spit at the Sheriff, who stepped to the side, missing the offense.

The Sheriff was then handed a small torch by his Deputy, and placed the burning end into the gathered wood, holding it there until smoke began.

The crowd audibly breathed out as flames began to flicker higher and higher.

Her screams carried well outside of the town limits, reaching the ears of Rebecca, rocking back and forth in her chair.

And so, on a cloudy morning, Rachel gathered her ingredients and made the earth shudder in fear at the ancient tongue spoken during the cast.

---

ON THAT MORNING, in 1690, Joseph and his wife Mary, along with their son George, made their way through the woods on their buggy. Their beloved horse Patches slowly pulled them along, while Joseph and Mary sat close to each other on the driver's bench, enjoying each other's touch.

Young George was in the back, tossing pebbles over the sides, laughing whenever one hit a tree.

As the buggy approached the hovel, unaware of the fury of Rachel within, unaware of the recent execution of Sarah, the riders and the horse felt a disturbance in the atmosphere around them, as the ingredients were tossed in. And as the cast was spoken, and the earth shuddered, Patches was startled. Hundreds of hares scurried from the bushes across the road in front of them.

Patches reared up unexpectedly, Joseph attempting to stop the mighty animal from creating havoc, but to not avail. Even pulling hard on the reins, the horse careened backwards, crashing down onto the buggy behind it, causing it to topple over in front of the three huts.

Within the hut, Rachel heard the crash, followed by the cries of pain. Not sure what was happening, she rushed outside, not disguising herself.

In front of her was a most bizarre scene. A young boy was standing near the gate. Behind him, a large horse was toppled over haphazardly, a splintered buggy laying below it. As she approached, she could see the body of a woman under the dead horse. Hearing a groan, she looked closer and spotted a man, trying to pull himself from underneath the animal.

She squatted down, not wanting to get too close, unsure if this was a trap or not. Unsure why the buggy had been mangled.

Joseph spotted the old lady and knew instantly what she was and where they were. Knowing his options, Joseph made one last plea.

"His name is George. Please, care for him and love him as my wife and I have done. He deserves a home, don't let the Magistrate send him away before my time ends. Please may I have your word?"

She could see that he was paralyzed, that he had lost a lot of blood. He didn't have long now.

"You know what I am?"

He nodded his head slowly, growing weaker by the second.

"Then I will take young George in, and Rebecca and I will raise him to be a fine boy. I give you my word he will not be corrupted, and we will raise him to respect life and to respect God. The black arts will not pass over to him, as I know you wish that, but can't bring yourself to say it aloud."

She turned to the boy, tears in his eyes, stunned by the carnage in front of him.

She knelt down, wiped some dirt from his face.

"Young George, be a good boy and kiss your father goodbye. He will always be there for you, in memory and spirit, but today his body will be travelling elsewhere."

Young George ran forward, kissing his father on his forehead, squeezing him hard in an embrace. When he finally let go, Rachel saw that Joseph was no more.

"Come young man, let your new Grandmother bring you in from the cold."

She pushed the boy towards the hut, opened the gate, and led him through. As they got to the door, the boy stopped, turned and took one last long look at what was left of his parents. Then the door opened and he stepped inside.

———

MOMENTS after the cast had been spoken, life in town changed for some folk.

The Magistrate was sitting at his table enjoying some tea, looking out of the big window. He felt a soft wind blow through the room, followed by a stinging pain in his head. As he tipped his head forward in agony, he noticed a wet feeling within his nose. Opening his eyes, he saw that his tea cup was filling with blood that poured from his nostrils.

As his house keeper entered the room, the Magistrate didn't have time to utter a single word. He slipped off from the chair and crashed to the floor, dead before the servant could make it over to him.

———

THE SHERIFF meanwhile was at the jail house, replaying the events of the public execution over in his head. He couldn't get the image of a beautiful young blonde he had spotted out of his mind.

"Hey William," he called out, yelling at his Deputy.

"Yeah boss?"

"Did you see that beautiful young lady at the execution of the Witch? She was walking near the back of the crowd."

"Yessir, I did. Hadn't seen her in many years, but I know I saw her once before. She was washing some clothes once down at the old mill. I was cutting through Donnie's back lot and spotted her. We talked for a bit."

"You did?"

"Yessir. Wasn't much," he replied, drinking slowly from his coffee cup, "But it stuck with me. I was drawn to her hard, like some force was pulling me in. Her eyes, I tell you what, her eyes looked me straight in the soul, made me second guess why I wasn't down there washing clothes with her."

"Well what did you two talk about?"

"I can't for the life of me remember most of it. I can see the events, and see her mouth moving, and feel my mouth move as I replied, but just everything was mush coming out. I do remember her telling me her name, and inviting me back for dinner sometime."

He said all of this with a smile on his face. Clearly he was lost in the memory of this gorgeous female hypnotizing him.

"What was her name William?"

"She said her name was Rachel. She said she was the middle of three sisters. I remember that clear as day. She said come for dinner some time, we live close by, just me and my two sisters. Rebecca is the oldest and Sarah is the youngest, then she put all of the wet wash into the basket and walked away. I just stood and stared, fixed to the ground, not able to move. Finally, I came to, my senses returning, and ran after her, but she was gone."

"Well William, she was there last night, and I have a feeling we burned her youngest sister Sarah."

"What makes you say that?"

"I saw the beautiful Rachel in the courthouse, and again at the square. I ran into Rebecca many, many years ago, in her actual state, not young. So my logic tells me Sarah killed Miss Abigail and Rachel is none too happy."

William let out a long whistle, indicating that this wasn't good news. The Sheriff just nodded.

---

THE BARD WAS JUST STARTING to tune his instrument, the barkeep cleaning in the back room. The strings were each struck, one at a time, and as the sound reverberated out from the body, the bard would tune the knob attached to it, changing the pitch as needed. He was on the third string when the front door of the tavern was blown wide open, wind gusting in, almost knocking him from his stool.

Looking around, he was surprised to see a black crow standing near the entrance, its eyes glistening in the dim light. The eyes were unnerving, and caused the bard to look away quickly, afraid of what would happen if he kept looking.

Slowly, he glanced back and was relieved to find the black crow was gone, but in its place was a beautiful blonde woman.

"Bard, do you know who I am?" The woman asked, floating towards him.

Nodding his head, he replied, "Yes, I believe I do."

"I am Sarah's older sister. Not the oldest, no not Rebecca. If I were Rebecca, you would have stopped breathing when the wind first blew in. My name is Rachel, and I am here to tell you that I hold no ill will towards you, nor do I blame you for Sarah's death. She was the curious one, the one who blinded you with cast and enchanted you with tongues. She brought it on herself with the jealousy that flowed out and ended Miss Abigail's life."

"Thank you, Rachel. That is most kind. I have been heartbroken since the day of Miss Abigail's death, truly. I loved Sarah. Even now, knowing that she didn't look like she did, and that she tricked me, I miss her. We enjoyed our time together so very much. I know my hurt isn't as bad as yours, but I do hurt. I also apologize for my reaction. When Miss Abigail began to… began to… when that happened, I blurted it out. I shouldn't have."

"Oh bard, I know you truly cared for her. I spied on you two and I saw how she looked at you, and you at her," Rachel said, taking the bard's hand in hers.

"You are allowed to hurt. I also have a favour to ask of you. I have recently come into care of a very young man, George is his name. I have promised his parents, who have passed away now, to take care of this boy, raise him, and not teach him our dark arts. I wanted to know if you would be willing to be a teacher for him. Teach him music, poetry and the rhythm of life, as only a bard can. I can pay you, and would be forever in your debt."

"I think that is something I can do. I would feel as though I am honouring Sarah's memory."

With that the two came to an agreement and Rachel left the tavern.

The bard breathed out a sigh of relief, knowing full well his life was spared.

---

As THE WIND made its way through the town, the cast that had been sent forth found its targets and dealt them a quick death.

The Deputy's wife was washing some linens, when she fell to her knees in agony. Soon blood poured from her nose, much like the Magistrate, before she toppled to the floor, dead before hitting it.

---

A WEEK after the Magistrate and the Deputy's wife had met an untimely end, two events took place on the same day, both on opposite ends of the situation playing out.

The first, was a new Chief Magistrate arriving in town. There had been rumours sent to the big city that witchcraft had happened, an execution had occurred and now the town was in upheaval. All of this led to the Magistrate on staff dying, and order needed to be restored.

The new Magistrate gladly accepted the nomination.

"I will return the town to the Godly state it should be, letting the Lord lead the way," he said as he entered the buggy, prepared to start the journey.

The second event was the bard arriving at the huts, ready to have his first session with George.

The bard found himself standing outside the gate, looking at three run down huts. He had heard many rumours over the years about the huts and the sisters who lived in them, and now here he was, voluntarily entering them. He noticed some movement in the hut to the far left, and thought he saw someone in the window. Before he could look closer, the middle hut's door creaked open and Rachel exited, slowly walking towards him. This was not the version of Rachel he had talked to in the tavern, agreeing to come teach the boy. No, this was the normal version of Rachel, a very old, very haggard woman. She had long stringy black and grey hair, and wore a thick sweater, with a skirt that flowed around her legs.

"Bard, welcome," she spoke, her voice causing the bard's skin to crawl.

"I trust you are fine with my appearance. If not,

please let me know, and I will transform. George awaits you inside, he is very excited to begin learning about music."

"Rachel, may I ask you a question?"

"Of course, anything."

"Is this a trap? Will I enter and never be seen again? I saw movement in the window in that hut there," he pointed at the third hut as he spoke, "and honestly, I am afraid."

"Bard. To be frank, if I wanted you dead you would already be dead. The Magistrate learned that lesson. We came to a deal and my word is bond. I made a deal with George's parents when they passed away, and will respect that deal with them too. My older sister, whom you saw in the window, is very anti-social. If you do see her, it would be best to just wave or say hello, but to keep moving on. Now I will give you this one-time option here. If you do not want to continue on, I ask that you do this one lesson, and then you are free to leave and never come back. George will be disappointed, but I can search elsewhere. Your life will be spared, and we will not be angered at you for your decision. I personally would greatly appreciate you teaching George, as I have had no children myself and this is strange territory for me. But, it is your decision and I will accept what you decide."

The bard appreciated the offer, but he knew he was also a man of his word, and having agreed before, and knowing now it wasn't a trap, he wasn't about to rescind.

"I respect your frankness, Rachel. Thank you. I am excited to teach George now, and for however long we continue to keep the lessons going. Shall we begin?"

Rachel nodded, and they walked towards the middle hut. As they got to the door, a creaking noise cut through the air, and movement at the third hut caused the bard to stop and look. It was the older sister, Rebecca, and her arrival caused the bard to freeze in place, slightly shaking with fear.

"Bard, thank you for teaching George."

She then re-entered into her hut, letting the bard breathe out in relief.

"Wasn't expecting that," Rachel muttered, as she opened her front door, letting the bard enter first.

What greeted the bard was most unexpected.

From the outside, a person wouldn't be wrong for believing the interior to be small and cramped. In truth, the interior was larger than expected, because it pushed deep under the hill it was nestled in. Tree roots poked out in a number of areas, but for the most part it was free of interference. There was a large kitchen area, a dining area and some doors, leading into bedrooms.

"Larger than you were expecting?"

"Why yes," the bard replied, still flabbergasted at the size.

"We each have land under the hill, so I went straight back, and my two sisters went sideways. We like the illusion of the small hut doors out front. Keeps strangers away."

"Very true." The bard hadn't seen George yet, which still made him feel a bit tense.

"George, come on out, your teacher is here."

From the back of the living room, one of the bedroom doors slowly opened. A small boy, no older than eight tip-toed out, a brown mop of hair covering most of his head.

The bard knelt down, bringing him to the same level as George, and smiled warmly.

"Hello George. Would you like to learn some music?"

The boy returned the smile, nodding his head excitedly.

"Does he speak?" the bard asked Rachel.

"Oh does he ever. Once you get him to open up, he won't stop. Nothing wrong with that, considering what he witnessed here, when his parents were crushed by the horse."

The bard flinched when he heard that. *His parents were crushed by a horse?*

"Well that doesn't sound too fun. Music though can help heal as well as bring joy. What shall we start with today? How about some joy?"

George nodded and jogged into the living room, sitting on one of the chairs. The bard stood up and Rachel motioned for him to join the boy.

The bard walked over, and then sat on the floor in front of the boy, crossing his legs. He pulled his instrument from his back, letting the strap lead it to his front. Then he strummed the strings, watching the boy's eyes light up.

The bard suddenly grabbed the strings, stopping the sounds the instrument made.

"George, have you ever heard music before?"

The boy stared back at the stranger, silent, mouth clenched tight.

"George, it's ok, you can talk to this man. The bard is

a friend. He was a great friend to your Aunt Sarah when she was alive."

"Ok," George whispered to her, making sure to not make any eye contact with the bard.

"Well, he asked you a question. It would be rude for you to not answer. Have you ever heard music?"

Her repeated asking of the question let his mouth loosen a bit.

"Just when my mother would sing to me," the boy said.

"Oh, that's great. Well then, you have heard some rhythm before. I think most people learn and enjoy music more when they are involved. Rachel, do you have any wooden spoons or anything George here can use to tap along?" The bard spoke quickly, trying not to scare the boy with his own excitement from music.

Rachel went into the kitchen and returned, producing a fine looking wooden spoon. She shuffled over, handed it to George, and then gave him a kiss on the head.

"Ok, George, I am going to sing a happy song, and play a happy tune. Now the key to music is to find the rhythm. It's the beat that makes the song advance. It's like your heart in your chest, the waters in the lake, or the sun shining on your face. So the song will go bah, bah, bah, bah. Ok? So tap the spoon with the rhythm. If you want to listen for a little bit, you can."

George nodded in acknowledgement.

The bard began to strum the instrument again, and after a few strums, began to sing a happy tune, specifically for the young boy.

*"There was a boy, a handsome young lad,*

*Who was known as George throughout the land,*
*He loved the sun, and the ocean deep,*
*He loved his friends, and going to sleep.*
*Then one day, he caught a wish,*
*Saw a star, and got a kiss,*
*George was smiling so, so wide,*
*Happy that he was alive."*

Half way through the tune, the young boy was tapping the spoon to the beat, and the second time he heard his name, he smiled, matching the song.

"How was that?" the bard asked.

"Fantastic! Aunt Rachel, did you hear the song? It was all about me and what I liked! He even sang my name twice! May we sing it again please?"

Rachel was in the kitchen, making bread, listening to the tune and then the banter afterwards.

"That's great, George, how nice."

"Of course," the bard replied, "we can sing this tune as many times as you want today, while I am here. When I sing it again, do you want to sing a few lines?"

"But I don't know the words yet?"

"You don't have to. For this song, you can make up whatever you want."

So the two started again, the bard strumming and singing, the boy tapping the spoon in time. When it got to the right point, the bard pointed to the boy and he sang two lines;

*"Rachel was so very kind, helping me stay in line,*
*I was so very scared, but she arrived just in time."*

The bard glanced at Rachel, still strumming the instrument, but didn't see any sideways glance.

"Great job, George! Way to think on your feet. Now here, let's spend some time with the instrument. You strum away and I will teach you some chords."

The two of them spent close to an hour playing with the instrument, while the bard taught the boy some chords, where to put his fingers, and how to change sounds.

Finally, it was time for lunch, so Rachel came over.

"Bard, you are most welcome to stay for some lunch if you would like. I have soup and bread prepared. If not, I would say it is time to end the lesson for today, and George and myself would be delighted if you came back the day after tomorrow. What say you?"

"That is a fine offer, but if it is no offence to you, I will head back to town. I must prepare for my appearance tonight at the tavern, and I have to prepare for a wedding this coming weekend. Today has been most enjoyable, and George you are already very talented, so I will see you both the day after tomorrow."

"Aye, sounds good. George, please show the bard to the door, and I will dish up our food."

The boy walked the bard to the door. The bard exited the hut, and walked to the road, closing the gate behind him. Turning, he saw the boy still at the door, and waved, smiling when the boy waved back.

---

In town, the new Magistrate was wasting no time.

He interviewed the Sheriff, the Deputy and as many of the patrons of the tavern from the night of Miss

Abigail's death as he could. He spent time at the small library, reviewing pertinent history, passed down over the years, about the family of witches living on the outskirts of town.

From this he found some interesting facts. While the town itself was a few hundred years old, there were records suggesting the three small huts had been there long before. A report from a neighbouring Magistrate indicated foul play from over 500 years ago, which they attributed to the family of witches living in the hovel.

The Magistrate also came across the reports of the mother and father being found guilty of supernatural acts, and being hung from a large tree.

While the Magistrate himself was a God fearing man, he wondered, after reading all of the facts and under-standing the three most recent deaths, if maybe the ideal course here wasn't more executions, but an agreement.

The safety of many was more important than the safety of a few, the Magistrate reckoned, and in this case, three people had already paid the ultimate price. If the Magistrate could persuade the family at the edge of town to leave them well enough alone, then just maybe the town itself could return to normality. Additionally, he thought that if he could negotiate a treaty with the group of witches, then maybe he could garner favour with the President.

---

As THE NEXT few weeks went by, the bard grew to look forward to the walk out to the small huts, as well as the music lessons. The first few times he had feared a bit for his life, but soon realized that Rachel and Rebecca had nothing but the best interests in the boy at heart, and that while they may be capable of horrible acts, they treated him with respect.

His time there had opened up a relationship with Rebecca that even Rachel didn't see coming. When the bard arrived, Rebecca would come out and make small talk with him, asking about the weather, what songs they would be performing and had even inquired about his family. It was now at the point that she made some cookies for him to bring to his parents, who returned the sentiment by sending some fresh bread with him.

All of this, though, filled the bard with some sadness, and he expressed as much to Rachel on one such visit.

"Seeing how nice you all are too me, and to young George, makes my heart ache. People won't spent the time to get to know you, they are all scared of you. But for me, it saddens me, because it makes me think of what could have been with Sarah. She would have been so elated to see all of us getting on so well."

"That she would. Sarah was a kind soul. What happened to her was awful and we will never forget it. Bard, I know you are growing complacent with Rebecca, but I must warn you. She doesn't have a kind heart."

The bard thought about what Rachel said the entire walk back to town that day, only breaking his concentration when a group of horses came riding up to him quickly.

"Hey Bard? Where are you coming from?"

The Deputy was leading the horse caravan, and the

bard could tell he wasn't asking this question with kindness behind it.

"If you must know, good Deputy, I am coming from a music lesson. I see a young boy named George two, sometimes three times per week, depending on my schedule."

"I don't recall no George in town, Deputy," a voice piped in. Turning, the bard saw it was Arthur. The bard at one time had been friends with Arthur, but when they boys became teenagers, the bard preferred music, while Arthur preferred trouble.

"He doesn't live in town, Arthur. He lives a short distance out. His family contracted me to teach him after seeing one of my performances at a birthday party. Not that any of this is your business, I have committed no offence to be stopped or questioned about. Now if you may, I need to continue to the tavern, I have a performance tonight that I must rehearse for."

The bard pushed through the crowded horses, beginning to walk away from the caravan, a bit more pep in his step. Hearing a whistle in the air, the bard was felled by a tremendous pain in his leg. When he attempted to pick himself off of the ground, he found he couldn't. Looking at his legs, he was alarmed to see a whip was around them, with the handle in the Deputies hand.

"I didn't give you permission to leave, bard."

The bard unwrapped the thick end of the weapon, and stood up, brushing the dirt from his trousers.

"Deputy, heed your temper now. I have done no wrong. I am willing to look beyond this, but another such outburst and I will go to your boss and the Magistrate."

The bard was shaking with worry, not sure what was going to happen next.

"Hit him again boss, don't let this *musician* walk away from us," Arthur said.

The Deputy appeared to agree with Arthur, and started to wind up the whip, when an elderly lady stepped from the woods.

"What's the meaning of this Deputy?"

The Deputy dropped his whip immediately, alarmed at the sight of this old woman.

"Be off woman. I mean no harm to you. This is between the law, the lord and the bard."

"Ha, ha, ha," the old woman burst out laughing, drawing concerned glances between the men on the horses.

"I see no law and no lord here. I see young Arthur, still scared about things under his bed at night. Look, bard, there's young Wilmot. He is scared too, but not about his bed. He is worried people will find out what he does with the family cat when no one is home. The other four of you, I won't waste the air in my lungs. As for you, Deputy. When you go to sleep at night, what do you see? Do you see your wife's body on the floor at home, you entering the house, that big pool of blood? Or do you see the flames burning bright, and the screams piercing the air?"

"WITCH!" The group hollered, horses rearing back.

The bard had recognized Rebecca as soon as she appeared from the side of the road, but now he was worried the horses would trample her. She was a very old lady and moved very slowly. He also recognized that he was in significant trouble now. These men would, in short order, tell the townsfolk that the bard had a relationship with the witches. He put that behind him momentarily. He knew priority one was to get Rebecca safely home, and then priority two was to report this incident to the Sheriff and the Magistrate.

Priority one, though, wasn't going to be an issue. As a few of the horses began to move towards Rebecca, a swirl of wind appeared in front of her, whipping around and around, knocking the animals backwards and over.

The Deputy wasn't about to have his friends and posse harmed by this witch. Putting his fingers in his mouth, he whistled sharply.

"Leave these two alone. Let's go boys, we will handle this shortly. Come," and with that he snapped his reins and was off, the horse galloping away. The others all followed his lead, and in a matter of seconds, the bard was left alone with Rebecca.

"Thank you, Rebecca. I'm not sure what the outcome would have been, if not for your arrival."

"Bard, you are most welcome. George speaks highly of you, and the Deputy needs to learn his place. Now, I understand I have put you in a bad spot. My suggestion would be to go and speak with the Sheriff at once. The Magistrate believes in a higher power, and won't be kind to your complaints."

Then Rebecca stepped into the branches, disappearing as quickly as she had appeared.

GEORGE WAS SITTING on the floor of his new home, playing with some wooden blocks. His music lesson had recently ended and while Rachel went and had a nap, he was entertaining himself. Suddenly he had a flash, a bright light going off in front of his eyes. When he opened them again, he could see his music teacher, the bard, walking on his way back to town, with a group of horses approaching. He knew the bard was in danger, so getting up, he ran next door, to Rebecca's place, and told her what he had witnessed.

"Boy, I love you, like you were my own flesh and blood, but we promised your parents we wouldn't teach you the dark arts. Rachel and I will discuss this after, but I will go and make sure the bard is ok. You return to the house and wait for me."

He waited, and watched as Rebecca left the yard, closing the gate behind her, and then walked into the trees, disappearing from view.

Not too long after, Rebecca entered Rachel's hut to find George playing with the blocks once again.

"Well done, young George. Your teacher was in fact in peril. Now, how did you do that? Speak, and be honest."

George hung his head low, not wanting to look up and make eye contact with her.

"Speak," she hissed at him, not wanting to resort to a cast of honesty.

"Aunt Rebecca, to be truthful, I can read really well. So sometimes, when Aunt Rachel has a nap, I will read the old books she has around here. I like my music teacher and the lessons are so much fun. I wanted to see where he lived, so I found a cast that was simple enough, and used it so that I could follow him home, but I guess when the horses approached, the cast forced me to see that instead. I'm very sorry. I didn't know my parents asked that. I won't do it anymore."

"Aye, I accept your apology. We will need to tell Rachel when she wakes up. We have created some trouble for the Bard, and we will need to determine our next steps. But for now, you did a good thing George, and you are a good boy."

Rebecca went over and squeezed him tight, giving him a kiss on his thick head of hair.

---

THE BARD WENT STRAIGHT into town, walking with a slight limp through the village square, where his dear Sarah had been burned, and up to the front steps of the jailhouse.

Strumming his instrument loudly, he kept playing, even as folks from nearby buildings came out to see what was happening. Finally the Sheriff emerged. The Deputy shuffled out shortly afterwards, making sure to keep most of his body hidden behind the Sheriff.

"Afternoon Bard. Who may we thank for this unannounced performance today?"

"Hello Sheriff," the bard replied, stopping his strumming, "we can thank the good Deputy behind you. For he was the one who attacked me earlier with a whip, surrounded by his friend Arthur and his other goons."

The Sheriff's eyes closed slightly when hearing this, and turned slightly, making eye contact with the Deputy.

The Deputy shrugged, indicating he didn't know what the musician was referring too.

"More details maybe," the Sheriff replied.

"Well Sheriff, I was returning from a music lesson I had provided for a young boy, when a group of horses rode up on me. I was then whipped around my leg and thrown to the ground."

"This true?" The Sheriff asked, half turning his head in the Deputy's direction.

"He ain't telling the whole truth Sheriff. He was out at the huts. Doing whatever with the Witch. One of them saved him."

"This true?" The Sheriff asked, turning now to face the bard again. He was aware of the growing number of townsfolk encroaching on their conversation, and wanted to end this quickly.

"Partly. I was out at some huts, teaching a young man music. I didn't see any Witch. A lovely older woman did arrive and shame the *boys* into stopping their assault on me, and it appeared to work."

"Bard, go to the tavern, I will come follow up with you shortly. William, inside, NOW!" The Sheriff barked at his Deputy, who turned and went in quickly.

"NOW FOR THE REST OF YOU. WE ARE THE LAW. LEAVE THIS BARD ALONE. I DON'T CARE WHAT YOU HAVE HEARD, OR THINK YOU HAVE HEARD, WE WILL DEAL WITH THIS ACCORDINGLY."

The bard nodded and turned, walking back towards the tavern, aware of the stares from the people.

RACHEL WAS NOT happy to find out about George and his extra reading. She understood why; a boy his age was curious by nature, but she was steadfast in her promise to his parents. George would not be trained in the dark arts, and would not ever have a firm grasp on cast or old tongues.

She also understood the boy wanting to see where the bard went each day, when he finished the lesson.

"Maybe, George, we can arrange for a time, where you can go and visit the bard. Does that sound like a good plan?"

George, who had been hanging his head in shame, popped up, his small face filled with a big smile.

"Oh yes please, that would be most amazing! I would be so well behaved, I promise."

Rachel had never felt as fulfilled as she did when she witnessed George's smile.

"How about this. I know he has a performance tonight. Let's ask Rebecca if she wouldn't mind the two of us heading into town, and we can watch him perform from outside. You are too young to be allowed in, but there are many places we can watch from, and you can see just what the bard gets up to. After the performance, we can ask the Bard if he can show you his house. Now don't get your hopes up. Rebecca dislikes the town and may say no. If she does say no, we stay, and the bard may also say no. He has his own life as well, so if he says no, then it doesn't happen. Understood?"

George nodded, the smile still glowing on his face.

STEVE STRED

Rachel was very surprised when Rebecca agreed to let them go.

The entire walk, Rachel had to work to get George to slow down, his excitement growing with each step.

"I've never been to town before," he said, "We were on our way when my parents died."

George's words made Rachel stop in her tracks. George had never mentioned his parents' death before. He had mostly remained quiet over the first few days at her place, before finally opening up and bit and talking to her.

"George, do you remember the accident?"

George kept walking, head lowered, before stopping, turning and looking at Rachel.

"We need to keep walking Aunt Rachel, I don't want to be late."

She wasn't about to push it, so she shut up and they kept walking.

Arriving at the edge of town, Rachel had George stop.

"George, I'm going to need to change how I look, to make sure no one suspects it's me. Would you like me to transform into a man or a woman?"

George thought about the question for a few moments before enthusiastically replying; "Woman!"

"Why's that George? You don't want me to be your Uncle for the night?"

"Nope. Girls are better."

To the point. So Rachel stepped into the bushes at the side of the path as herself, and walked back onto the path

86

as a young woman, ready to go listen to some music from the bard.

---

THE BARD HAD WALKED QUICKLY to the tavern, aware of how much the townsfolk scrutinized him with their eyes. It hadn't been ideal to bring this much attention to himself, but he knew that was the only way the Sheriff would listen to his grievances, especially after being assaulted by the Deputy.

Arriving at the tavern, he went to his spot behind the stage and started to tune and clean his instrument, when he heard the front doors swing open.

Looking out from behind the curtains, he was surprised to see the Sheriff was already there.

"Sheriff, that was quick. Am I to assume that I need to follow you back to the jailhouse?"

The Sheriff walked towards him, shaking his head side to side.

"No, Bard, I spoke with the Deputy, with William. He admitted as much about what you said. Now I just need to confirm something. The old lady, was she a witch?"

"Sheriff, I know what happened with Sarah, my deceased. But when an old lady had to defend me from a group of thugs on horses, it's frustrating to think the only explanation is that she was a witch."

"I hear you. Just had to ask. Bard, if you have any further trouble, let me know."

Then the Sheriff left, leaving the musician alone.

---

WILLIAM WAS BEYOND ANGRY, and once the Sheriff left, after yelling at him for assaulting the musician, he kicked his desk hard. Hard enough to knock the chair over beside it.

Arthur came in, seeing the chair on the floor and whistled sarcastically, which prompted the Deputy to tell him to shut up.

"Now, now, I'm still your friend. We need to teach that Bard a lesson. Make him pay for being in cahoots with those witches."

"Arthur, you are right. The Sheriff can't see clearly, which makes me wonder if he isn't also working with that group. Maybe the witches have a deal with him. I think the best route here is for me to assume control of this here jailhouse and let's go arrest that Bard. Arthur, I am making you my Deputy for the time being. Let's go!"

The two of them set off for the tavern, wanting to arrive when the music began.

---

THE MAGISTRATE WAS HAVING similar thoughts. For him, the connection between all of the goings on in town was with the Bard. Setting off for the tavern, he wanted to question the minstrel and find out what the truth was.

---

RACHEL, George, the Magistrate, the Deputy (acting as Sheriff), and Arthur (acting as Deputy), all arrived at the tavern, just as the music began. The Bard was onstage and introduced himself to the crowd, before strumming his instrument and playing a lovely tune that he dedicated to his parents.

Rachel and George were standing off to the side of the stage, outside of the tavern, enjoying the show through the open windows. There were barstools pulled up for them to sit on, and George was grinning wildly, bobbing his head along. Rachel found herself tapping her feet along as well.

The Magistrate stood near the middle of the room, looking around at the patrons, trying to spot anyone who looked out of place. The child and the lady outside at the window caught his attention, but as he didn't know many folks yet, he wasn't sure if they should be investigated more.

The Deputy and Arthur stormed in, yelling for the music to stop and the Bard to put his instrument down, which he decided to ignore and continue playing, not accepting William as any authority after the assault on the roadway.

"What is the meaning of this? I am the authority here," the voice boomed, and hearing the thunder from within this man's chest, the bard immediately stopped playing, lowering his instrument.

The Magistrate had turned and was facing the Deputy and Arthur.

"I said, what is the meaning of this?"

"Sorry, who are you?" Arthur spoke up, having not met the new head of justice in the town.

"I'm the appointed Magistrate, approved by the high court of the country through God himself. That is who I am. Who, pray tell, are you?"

Arthur, upon hearing the man's title, shrunk, realizing this was a battle he did not wish to be a part of.

While this scene was starting, Rachel said a quick low cast, and sent it towards the Bard, drawing his attention. The bard, seeing her first but not recognizing her, started to turn his head back to the scene at hand, when he did a double take, realizing the young boy with this lady was his pupil. George waved at him, beckoning him to come over, and the bard obliged, leaving the stage as inconspicuously as he could.

"Rachel? Is that you?"

"Yes Bard, it is. Now come, we must get you out of here, this won't end well for you."

The bard didn't need to be told a second time, and as the Magistrate boomed behind him, the bard snuck through the side door, heading outside with the woman and the boy.

"Bard, it is unsafe for you to return with us, people will be watching. Head to your place and stay there, leaving the lock shut tight. I will send a message in the next day or so, once I have a better understanding of how this all plays out."

The bard simply nodded and rushed away into the ever darkening night, wanting to get home and be safe behind lock and key.

Inside, the Magistrate stood barrel chested, ego puffed up, ensuring that everyone knew he was in charge.

"I'm sorry Magistrate, I was just acting accordingly. I suspect that the good Sheriff may be aiding the witches, and playing favourites with the Bard. So I have assumed control of the jailhouse, acting now as Sheriff, and my good friend here, Arthur, has been assigned to act as my Deputy."

The Magistrate let out a loud huff at the Deputy as he finished speaking.

"I give you no aid in this unjust coup of the jailhouse and the badge of the Sheriff. You are no Sheriff, nor are you a Deputy. Surrender your badge, your handcuffs and your keys to the jailhouse. I officially relieve you of your duty to the town and to your God."

Arthur began to speak, when William cut him off.

"I accept your decree Magistrate," he said, handing him his badge, handcuffs and jail keys, "But know this. The Bard was in bed with a witch. I watched her burn on the stake in the town square. He turns his eye to our town, desiring to play with the dark arts. God won't look kindly on him, nor will God look kindly on you, sir, for letting him go without so much as a slap on the wrist."

William turned, grabbing Arthur, and walked out of the tavern. Arthur began to speak again, before William cut him off, and pointed.

"That's one of the witches, and the boy. Quietly now, we must follow."

HEARING A COMMOTION, the Sheriff returned to the tavern, displeased to be greeted by the Magistrate. After being filled in, he asked where the musician was.

"I saw him flee," one of the patrons spoke up. "He spoke to some woman and a child, then he hurried away in one direction, while the other two headed away in the opposite."

"Thank you," the Sheriff said to the witness, "Anyone else see anything?"

"I saw William and Arthur follow the woman and the boy. They were keeping a bit of distance," another witness remarked.

This troubled both the Sheriff and the Magistrate, knowing full well that William and Arthur were seeking revenge.

---

THE BARD MADE it back to his small living space, locking the door first thing. He was on edge, constantly pacing around, peeking out of his window, expecting a group of people to be congregating below, flames burning high, yelling for his head.

None of this happened. Finally all of the excitement tired him out, and as he sat on his bed, his eyes grew heavy, he laid down on his side, and fell fast asleep.

---

RACHEL AND GEORGE made it back to the small hut, and had closed the door behind them, when outside, the yelling started.

"George, run along, go play in your room. It has been a long day, but you can stay up a bit longer. I just need to take care of this disturbance, and then we will get you ready for bed."

Although George wanted to see what would happen, he understood and walked back to his room, closing the door behind him.

Rachel went and looked out of the window, spotting William and Arthur on the roadway. They, much like the other locals who would make the trip, were always too scared to actually open the gate and walk towards the huts, but this time, they were standing at the fence, hurling insults at them. She knew it was all a way to try and get a rise out of her, but she would be fine. Calm and cool.

Rebecca on the other hand, may not take too kindly to the loud annoyance.

"Get out here now, so that God can judge thee!"

"This is your last chance! Exit now or burn for your sins!"

The door to the third hut slowly opened, causing William and Arthur to stop their yelling and take a step backwards.

"Who's there?" William asked, the space between the frame still dark and shapeless.

A dark cloud started to slowly spill out of the opening, starting at the bottom and silently slithering across the ground towards the fence.

"William, I don't know about this," Arthur said, voice cracking, taking another step backwards.

"Hold tight coward, this is clearly a tactic to have us flee, not inflict any harm towards the vile demon within."

"NO DEMONS HERE!"

A voice boomed through the night, causing the two to flinch and duck, as though thunder had cracked directly above their heads.

The dark cloud finally arrived at their legs, and as Arthur had stepped back, circled around William's legs first. It took a moment before he began to scream, pain searing through his legs, as the acid cloud ate through his thick trousers, then devoured his flesh and finally went through his bones, causing him to fall to the ground, legs amputated from the ankles down. Unfortunately for William, he fell forward, landing in the black fog, and began screaming again as it ate through his forearms and legs. With each new amputation, he pitched forward further, before finally his head fell into the cloud of death, and he went silent.

Arthur was frozen. The cloud of black had stopped at William, and retreated as soon as he had been dissolved. Soaking back into the third hut, the door slowly closed after it, leaving him alone, standing outside of the huts.

The sounds of horses arriving made Arthur scream out loud, but quickly shut his mouth when the Magistrate and Sheriff arrived, neither looking all too happy.

"Arthur, where is William?" The Sheriff questioned.

"He's... a cloud... black... screaming so loud... there... I," he stammered, pointing at the hut, then pointing at the ground, the last resting place of William.

"Get it together Arthur, God himself gives you strength. Now where is the Deputy?" The Magistrate knew the stories and did not want to be added to the town's dark history.

"The door. The door opened, and a cloud. A black cloud came out and ate William. The witch! The witch killed William!"

The Sheriff couldn't hide his disdain for this reply, rolling his eyes heavily, but when he looked over at the Magistrate, his mood soured, realizing that this man believed whole-heartedly what Arthur was saying.

He needed to simmer this quickly, before the Magistrate took things too far in the wrong direction.

"Arthur, take a breath here. Let's look at this reasonably. First off, why are you out here?"

Arthur was taken aback with the question. He didn't want to implicate himself, so he tried to deflect the attention.

"I just followed William."

"Sure you did," the Sheriff replied, frustrated with being out here. "So where is the Deputy?"

"I already told you, he was dissolved."

"Sheriff, step down, let a trained hand ask the harder questions," the Magistrate said, asserting himself over the Sheriff.

"Arthur, what did the witch look like?"

"A black cloud. Just a thick black cloud that came from the hut and ate William."

"Arthur, get a hold of yourself," the Sheriff snorted, fed up. "I get that William is angry, but to bring you into this nonsense is a bit much."

"I swear, Sheriff, I'm telling the truth."

"Sheriff, steel yourself here. Do not tread lightly on matters of the Lord. I believe this lad," the Magistrate said, chest puffing up even more.

As the Sheriff prepared to offer a rebuttal, the air was sliced by the sound of a door creaking open. All three men stopped and turned, the Sheriff and the Magistrate feeling their horses clenching up.

The door to the third hut slowly opened, but this time the darkness in the frame was chased away by first the silhouette, then the outline of a very old woman. Rebecca appeared from the shadows, and shuffled to the end of the walkway, stopping at the gate.

"SHUT UP! Won't the three of you be respectful and shut up already? First this blathering ninny shows up, yelling at us, then you two arrive on your horses, clomping around, telling each other that they are wrong and the other is correct. How about this. I am old, and I want to sleep. So either charge this young man with harassment, or be off with you three, so I may return to sleep."

Rebecca then turned, slowly starting to shuffle back to the hut, when the Magistrate spoke.

"Stop right there. This man says he was here with the Deputy, and that you used witchcraft to dispose of him. What say you? Are you a witch?"

Rebecca turned, faster than the three expected, all pulling back at the sight of her exposed face, hair flipping away.

"Did you just call me a witch? So first this man comes and disrespects me, yelling obscenities at me, and now you, a supposed Magistrate, would disrespect one of his elders. What would your Mother say? Or what would your Grandmother say? Shame on you."

She turned again and began to leave, a smile on her face.

"My apologies," the Magistrate replied, not happy that she was walking away. "Come now, Arthur, hop on up behind me, and the three of us will leave this woman be."

Arthur, helped by the Magistrate, hopped behind the man and the two horses now turned and began to head back into town. Half way there the Magistrate stopped.

"What is the meaning of this stoppage?" The Sheriff prompted, unsure what the Magistrate had in store.

"Sheriff, when I was coming through law school, we were told a Latin saying; 'Noli me tangere', which means 'don't touch me' or 'don't cling to me'. I believe that the witch we just encountered was expressing 'noli me tangere' to us right now. She first used an attack to dissolve the good Deputy, then deflected attention away, in order to prompt us to leave. Now, you take Arthur back to the village, I am going to walk back and see if I can't spot some evidence that not only links that lady to the Deputy's disappearance, but also corroborates my theory that she is a witch."

The Sheriff was beside himself.

"Your Honour, I understand you are the acting Magistrate, and we are thankful to have someone as experienced as yourself, but saying that, and with all due respect, that idea is both disrespectful to the old lady as well as asinine in its presumption. I have been privy to many stories over the years, and I myself ordered the execution of the recently convicted witch, but I do not believe the disappearance of my Deputy to be related to a so-called witch. I beg of you, return with myself and with young Arthur, and leave well enough alone."

The Magistrate listened, all the while slowly and silently nodding his head. Once the Sheriff finished, the Magistrate looked directly at the Sheriff, making firm and uncomfortable eye contact, before speaking.

"Sheriff, I have nothing but respect for you, and have heard admirable reports from this area for many a year. Of you being a strong, firm but just Sheriff, one who appreciates the law, but will take the time to hear the human side of events. Saying all of this, and again, with all due respect, but your comments to me, make me see you in a different light. Your diatribe sounds like someone attempting to hide or protect someone. In this case, it disturbs me, as it sounds like you are trying to protect a witch. Tell me good Sheriff, are you working against God? Are you putting witchcraft over the word of the Lord?"

The Sheriff was startled by the Magistrate's words, and was not in any mood to deal with this ridiculous accusation.

"Magistrate, I humbly tell you to stuff your words back down your throat. Arthur, let's go, let's leave this buffoon on his own, where he can go back, and disturb an elderly woman, one who has already been disturbed enough tonight."

The Sheriff declined to give the Magistrate time to reply, instead kicking the sides of the horse hard, galloping off into the darkness quickly.

The Magistrate rode back, stopping close to the huts,

before getting off of his horse and tying it to a tree. Slowly he walked to the gate at the end of the walkways, feeling a rush of adrenaline as he approached.

A noise alerted him, and looking up he was surprised to see a big, black crow, which flapped its wings hard, before landing on a post on the gate.

The eyes of the bird pierced the Magistrate, in a way that unsettled him to his core. Reaching up slowly, he grabbed the cross that he wore, always sitting heavy around his neck.

"Avis auferat," he said, saying *away bird*, in Latin, but to no success. Instead the bird shimmied across the top of the fence, its talons clicking against the wood.

"Auferetur daemonium!" the Magistrate now shouted, *away demon*, hoping to connect with it. The bird let out a squawk and took off, hissing at the man as it departed.

"I knew it," he whispered to himself, clutching the cross harder. His hand was shaking, when a new noise drew his attention. This time the noise was coming from behind him.

Turning slowly, grasping harder at this sacred crucifix he wore, he let out a quick, sharp gasp of air when he spotted the black goat. Horns long and rounded, curving back and away from its face.

"Daemonium!" he cried, as the animal huffed and dug its hoofs into the ground, kicking dirt out behind it.

"Christus adiuva me," he squealed, *Christ help me*, as the goat charged. As the animal got within a few feet, it transformed into a large winged beast, before the Magistrate was engulfed in its wings, screaming in agony.

The sounds didn't last long.

The darkness covering the man soon turned into a mist, and slowly floated over to the door of the third hut. As the door creaked slowly open, the mist shifted back into the shape of the goat.

"Come in," Rebecca called from inside, and the goat entered, the door closing behind it.

———————

THE SHERIFF and Arthur had made quick time returning to the jail house, but it didn't mean the Sheriff was happy. Once they arrived, they headed inside, Arthur on his heels like a puppy.

"Arthur, I can't even begin to tell you how angry I am."

"I know, I am sorry."

"Come over here, sit down," the Sheriff said, leading the young man to a bench. Once Arthur sat down, the Sheriff turned, and closed the cell door behind him, locking it with a loud THUNK.

"Hey, what's the meaning of this?" Arthur pleaded.

"Son, you deserve a punishment. I need to determine the charges to write up, but until I know what happened to my Deputy, and until the Magistrate returns with his findings, you can sit right there and stew over your poor decisions."

Arthur didn't protest, just slumped over on the bench, starting to cry.

The Sheriff sat and waited, and waited some more, wondering when the Magistrate would return. As dawn broke and there was still no sign of the man, the Sheriff decided enough was enough. He walked over, kicking the metal cell, waking Arthur up.

"Get up boy, I need to go look for the Magistrate. I ain't letting you out, but if someone should come in, tell them I will back by noon."

The Sheriff then left, leaving before Arthur could comment back.

———

THE BARD AWOKE REFRESHED, stretching tall, before remembering the events of the previous night. He hadn't received any news from Rachel yet, but he decided he didn't want to wait inside any longer.

Unlocking the door, he headed down the steps, appearing out on the street below. He wanted to head to the tavern, find out what had occurred and if he still had a job there.

He walked only a few short paces before someone called his name.

Turning, he saw that it was the tavern owner, jogging to catch up to him.

"Morning sir, how was the night?"

"Just fine Bard, me thinks you made a wise decision leaving when you did. The Magistrate and the Sheriff left shortly after, but I think if you would have stayed you would be waking up in the jailhouse this morn, instead of in your own bed."

"Just as I thought. You know I am not a Witch, or involved in witchcraft, right?"

The tavern owner stopped walking, and grabbed the minstrel on his shoulders, pulling him off the street.

"Bard, no, I don't believe so. But keep your tidy mouth shut of such happenings. The less you say the less they have to hang you with. Understood?"

The bard nodded, and pretended to lock his mouth shut with a key.

"Aye, that won't work Bard, I still need your pretty voice to bring in the drunks and women!"

The two men burst out laughing, continuing to walk to the tavern.

———

THE SHERIFF WAS ALMOST ALL the way to the huts, when rounding a corner, he spotted the Magistrate's horse, still tethered to the tree from last night.

*Not good*, he thought, *not good at all*.

He decided to dismount, and tied his horse up next to the Magistrate's.

He walked slowly, but purposefully, towards the hut, feeling like every step was one step closer to a discovery. A discovery he did not want to make.

What lay before him, when he arrived was the furthest thing from his mind.

A young boy was playing in the yard while a black goat was eating grass nearby. Every once in a while, the boy would run over, and hop over the goat's back, causing it to kick out a bit, but not hitting the boy. In front of the second hut, an elderly woman, different from the one from the night before, was rocking in a rocking chair, appearing to be knitting something.

"Hello Sheriff," the old woman yelled out, well before he had made himself visibly known.

"Ahoy, how does the sun shine on you today?"

"Oh, don't be so flattering. I'm old and ugly and you burned my sister. You here for answers on your Deputy or your Magistrate?"

The Sheriff stopped in his tracks, unprepared for such a blunt reply.

"Well, if you are in a talking mood, how about both?"

"Such a pity. Sometimes, leaving well enough alone would solve so many issues in this world. I ask, before I answer, has the Bard been harmed?"

Once again the comments sidelined the Sheriff.

"As far as I know, the Bard is unharmed. I was at the jailhouse for the rest of the night, and no reports came in. So, to the best of my knowledge, he is just fine. Now, I don't know if this is a stall tactic, but get on with your answer, I beg of you."

The Sheriff didn't want to come off as pleading, but his voice had softened as he spoke.

"That boy, Arthur, was correct about your Deputy. He was dispatched. As for the Magistrate, you should ask the goat here about what happened. He has first-hand knowledge about the events."

She began to laugh, a deep, guttural laugh. A laugh so unsettling, the Sheriff believed that if he had ate breakfast that very morning, it would be spewing forth.

He looked over at the boy, at the goat, and didn't know how to proceed.

Turning back to the old woman, he fell to his knees. In her place was a beautiful young woman. She stood up, and sauntered towards him, dress flowing, hair cascading down, eyes locked on his.

"This can't be true, witchcraft doesn't exist. I am just a Sheriff, assigned to enforce our laws."

He began to weep, and now fell to all fours, his hands hitting the ground. As he wept, he felt something beside his left hand, and picking it up, he saw it was a cross. He recognized it instantly; the Magistrate's cross.

Looking up, the young woman had made it to the gate. She turned, and whistled lightly, the goat coming over.

"George, run along inside."

"Ok, Aunt Rachel," the boy replied, hurrying inside. When the door closed, the Sheriff, who was watching the boy go, began to plead for his life.

"No such luck today, law-man," the woman replied.

The gate opened, the goat charged, and all that was left was a badge and a cross.

———

THE BARD PLAYED THAT NIGHT, the crowd large and exuberant. When the set was over, he looked for the boy, or for Rachel, but didn't spot them.

The next day, he made the trip out to the huts, and was relieved to see George and Rachel in the yard, the boy playing with a large, black goat.

"Hello!" he yelled as he arrived.

"Bard, great to see you," Rachel replied, and George ran over, opening the gate for him.

"Bard, come in, we have some business to discuss before the lesson begins."

George walked in front of the bard, and once inside, Rachel closed the door behind them.

"Bard, this will be your last lesson. Things have shifted within the town and we believe the time to hibernate is now. So if you may, teach young George what you were planning to teach, then be off, and simply forget about us."

The Bard wasn't expecting this reception, but he knew better than to argue, or to try and extract more details from Rachel.

So he gave George his last lesson, and when it was over, he handed his instrument to the boy.

"Here, keep it. Play with your heart and play with your soul, and when your fingers hit the strings, think of me every so often."

The boy smiled the biggest smile of his life, and hugged the musician.

"Oh thank you bard, thank you! Aunt Rachel, look!"

"That is very kind of you bard. Now, the time has come, the lesson is over. We ask that you leave."

"I understand. Take care of yourself, George. You as well Rachel, I hope we may meet again, even if it is just in my dreams."

With that the bard left, and as he closed the gate behind him, he started to walk, before kicking something. Looking down, he spotted a cross. He reached down, grabbed it and then stood up, studying the heavy item. As he did, he was suddenly startled, as the goat pummelled itself into the fence, the noise causing him to jump.

"Ok, ok, I am leaving," the bard said, quickly walking away.

He walked away, leaving the three small huts behind him. A short distance later, he had a weird feeling in the pit of his stomach. Turning and walking back to the clearing, he saw that the huts were no longer there, and now there was no sign of a fence. Where the huts were, in their place, was just a dirt hill, underneath three thick trees.

---

THE NEXT FEW months was a period of calm and quiet in the town. A new Magistrate was appointed, and through him, a new Sheriff as well.

The bard found the tavern to be fuller than usual most nights, and when he asked the tavern owner about it, he had a simple reply.

"People will turn to music to return their joy, after a period of grief."

---

A FEW YEARS WENT BY, and the bard's curiosity finally got the best of him.

On a warm summer's day, he made the walk out to the location, formally home to the three small huts. He was a bit saddened when he saw that it was still just a hill.

From inside the hill, George watched the bard, wishing that he could leave and say hello to his friend.

"I know Georgie, I know. He was a good guy, loved your Aunt Sarah. But the time has come. I let him live a longer life than the others. My cast was set in motion and was carried by the wind of Mother Earth."

Rachel walked away, leaving the teenager standing, looking outside.

As the bard began to turn and leave, George pulled the instrument that had been gifted to him around his body and strummed the strings, sending a gentle chorus out of the hut.

Outside, the bard, retreating back towards the village, heard the noise and felt the vibration of the music through his soul, and smiled.

Walking away, he whistled a tune that he had taught to George, remembering the good times during the lessons.

Rounding a corner, he saw movement ahead, causing him to pause.

"Hello?"

He looked around, not seeing anything. A noise above him, caused him to look up, and he saw a large, black crow fly away, leaving the branch it had been perched on shaking.

*Must have been the bird*, he thought, and started to walk again.

Again, he caught movement ahead on the trail, and came to a stop.

Squinting, he peered into the trees at the edge, trying to make out what he was seeing. From the shadows, a large black goat stepped forward, kicking at the ground, head swinging wildly, horns cutting the air.

The bard recognized it immediately.

"I thought I had been respectful," he said out loud, "I'm truly sorry she died."

As he spoke, he dropped down onto his knees, facing the goat.

The animal huffed and chuffed, raking the ground with its hoofs.

"I'm sorry, Sarah," the Bard said, closing his eyes as the goat charged.

## END

# THE WITCH - ABOUT

'The Witch' was an afterthought originally. For my second collection 'Left Hand Path: 13 more tales of black magick,' I originally had my novellas 'Wagon Buddy' and 'Yuri' as stories in it. When I was going through my re-reads I found that those two stuck out so much as individuals that they deserved their own proper releases. 'Wardrobe Malfunction' replaced one, but I still wasn't sure what story to use to replace the other. Going through my WIP folder, I found the outline of my story about a musician who falls in love with a witch, only he doesn't know she's a witch. I dove back in and worked on expanding it and while writing it, I used a number of descriptions and lines that were noted within the Salem Witch trials in various pieces, be it from testimony, journals etc. I enjoyed adding these elements of the "real" witch hunt in my own witch hunt.

'The Witch' turned out to be possibly the best story in

that collection, or the one most people seem to reference when I see new reviews. My friend, Miranda, always asked about returning to that world. I knew I would return at some point.

I ended up returning twice, which you can read for yourself over the next two stories.

## 6

# THE TREE

## (THE WITCH PART 2)

The goat charged.

It struck the Bard square in the chest, knocking him to the ground. Then it was on him, kicking and goring, trying to pierce his chest, his stomach.

Someone yelled, the goat fled.

---

THE BARD FOUND himself bandaged and, in his bed, sore but better off than expected. A man was sitting in the chair by the door but stood when he saw the Bard groan.

"You're awake."

"And alive," the Bard replied.

"Barely. You're lucky I came along when I did."

"For that, I thank you."

"Stay away from there. They don't want you back."

By the time the Bard looked to the man, he'd already fled.

---

THIS WASN'T RIGHT.

The Bard stared at the mound where the sister's huts had been, wondering just where they'd gone.

He could've sworn that he heard music from somewhere, but all he saw when he looked was a dirt mound.

He'd been warned to never return, but he needed to see with his own eyes.

The Bard left, vowing to never come to where his love had lived again, where the deception burned the most.

---

LIFE WENT on for The Bard, for the next decade.

He played on his lonely stage, looking for Sarah in dark corners during every performance. The Bard hadn't understood the depth of his grief, the heaviness of sorrow that sat on his chest. Until one day, he woke and found his hands had palsied into fists and he was unable to play his instrument.

---

BY MID-AFTERNOON, The Bard, gripped in the throes of anger, found himself back at the place where the three sisters had once resided.

He fell to his knees, arms raised high above as he screamed and yelled until his throat was raw.

"I know this was you! Why? Why do this to me? Have I not honored Sarah? Have I not been a friend to you three?"

But no answer came.

He stood, knees cracking as he made his way to his feet.

The Bard turned in a circle, looking for anything, any sign that his pleas had been heard. He saw nothing that spoke to him, no crows, no goats, no animals of any species.

"George? George, you in there?"

He wanted to walk to where the hovel used to house the doors. Something held him back, as though the dirt was tainted or that his feet would burn.

The faded strains of a guitar being strummed tickled his ears but was muted by the dirt.

The Bard knew it.

George was still in there, still looking out through the glamor.

"George! Please? Look at my hands. Is this because I loved Sarah? Held her hands? Why? I am nothing without my music."

The Bard was sobbing now, staring at his clenched hands. He couldn't open them, extend his fingers, but his hands were clenching tighter from his rage, his fingernails digging into his palms so viciously that blood began to leak and drip to the ground.

The pain grew to be unbearable, the Bard screaming in agony.

That act was what forced the foggy haze of the spell to lift. The three doors appeared, shimmering and other-worldly, and there was George, rushing to aid the Bard.

George placed his hands on the Bard's, his clenched fingers extending upon contact. The Bard looked at his former student seeing that the years had moved along for the boy as well. Now, before him was a man. George had an unkempt beard and the corners of his eyes housed the creases of time and worry.

"Come inside, old friend. Before your screams reach the townsfolk."

Entering the cottage in the hill, the Bard was trans-ported back in time. The smell was the same, must blan-keted by a veil of dampness and dust. The kitchen was cluttered, the sink stacked with dishes. The area looked as though it had long been neglected.

"I know."

The Bard's eyes met George's, his former pupils moist.

"Is she ... gone?"

The Bard hadn't expected to sound so defeated, the quiver catching him off guard.

George grasped him in an embrace, and they hugged with shared sorrow.

After moving apart, George nodded and went to sit on a chair. Pulling a second out at the table, the Bard joined him and sat.

"How? When? I don't understand. I loved Sarah. I really did. I never believed I'd see her again, but a part of me believed she'd live forever. Somehow."

George took the Bard's hand in his, squeezing gently.

"Let me get some salve for those wounds. Then, I'll

share what has gone on here and why your hands did what they did."

---

THE PASTE that George applied generously to his palms stung, but the Bard knew it was needed.

They stood and looked through the grime covered window, out over the former front yard.

"You were our source of hope, of light," George began. "Rebecca spoke so highly of you. Always did. Sarah made a mistake, but even as a young man, I know she loved you. After Rebecca made the decision that it was best to ban you, to glamor the hovel and prevent anyone from seeing we still lived here, it was a turning point. While one year would go by 'out there' five would go by in here. The spell casted down on us, from within worked its way into our bones, our cells, and I watched as I aged while Rebecca broke down day by day, piece by piece."

George shook his head, remembering the worst, before walking to the living room. He bent and picked up something, a smile on his face when he turned and displayed his treasure to the Bard.

The guitar.

He strummed it once, twice, letting the sound fade into the ether.

"I kept at it, my teacher. Until my heart hurt too bad and my soul cried for me to stop. All alone now, I just can't bring myself the desire to create."

The Bard smiled. He understood.

He longed to grasp the instrument, but even thinking about it now caused his hands to burn.

"Come. Out back. I'll show you Rebecca as she exists now."

The Bard followed George through the house, arriving at a hidden door along the back wall. The Bard knew he'd have never found this door if not directed, it blended into the wall so very well.

George turned the rusted handle, pulled the door open. Behind it, leading from the house, was a dirt tunnel. Roots hung from the ground above. George led him through the tunnel, exiting a few hundred meters away, into a marshy area set back in the woods.

There, standing alone before the two, was a crooked tree with gnarled branches. Not a leaf adorned it, leaving it bare and bleak.

The Bard gasped at what he saw.

There she was.

*Rebecca.*

---

THEY STOOD.

The sun crossed the sky growing from bright to dim, warm to cool.

Animals of the forest came and went, keeping their distance from where the tree rested.

They sobbed, they laughed, they mourned.

Rebecca had been many things, but to these two solitary men she'd been more than they'd realized.

"She gave up, my friend," George said, as they turned

to make their way back to the tunnel. "She was unhappy with how the public had turned on her and her kind. So, she came here and laid down to rest. This tree grew from her remains."

The Bard took one last look at the tree before hurrying to catch up. George closed the door, the temperature immediately rising once shut.

"The day the final leaf fell, was the day Rebecca was truly gone. That was the same day your hands clenched. Our hearts had a connection. That connection severed."

The Bard understood. He would need to grieve and when he had finally accepted his loss his hands would let him play again.

"Will I ever see you again, George?"

"I think not. Our time has come to an end. When you leave, I'll be joining Rebecca. I have nothing left to give and can no longer live behind this spell."

The Bard nodded, then pulled George in for a final hug.

He left the cottage, leaving that part of his life in the past.

---

THE BARD NEVER MOVED AWAY.

Dark nights and cold days pushed the thought into his head, but he remained.

Partly due to stubbornness, partly due to heartbreak.

He left his position at the tavern, what use was a bard who couldn't strum their instrument?

A farmer saw him, wandering forlornly through the streets one eve, offering him room and board.

The Bard stayed on at the farm for another fifteen years, helping when and where needed.

———

ONE MORNING, the Bard awoke only to find a guitar at the end of his bed.

His rigid fingers wouldn't allow him to pick it up, strum its strings. So, he sat and admired the instrument, while the sorrow that constricted his heart whispered, *'it's time.'*

He went and found the farmer, himself now an old man longing for his youth, to tell him it was time he went on his way.

"You've been as loyal to me as my own son," the farmer said, patting the Bard on the arm.

The two shared a nod, before the Bard left him there, sitting in front of the farmhouse.

———

THE BARD STROLLED into town that fine day.

He'd not visited since he moved to the farm.

He found that nothing had changed, the streets had grown old and tired.

He walked past the tavern, the old sights, sounds and smells only ghosts of his memory. The place long boarded up and crumbling. *Was it his leaving that precipitated the downfall?*

The Bard didn't look back. Instead, he visited the places that meant the most to him and Sarah, each one bringing a smile to his face.

When the sun began to set, he continued on his way.

---

WHEN THE BARD arrived at the hovel, the first tear fell from his eye.

No huts greeted him, and he wondered just how he was going to find the tree that had grown out of Rebecca's remains.

The caw of a crow caught his ear and he saw the dark bird swoop low and make eye contact, all the sign he needed to follow.

They made their way down the road, circling around the area formerly housing the sisters, before the Bard spotted a path leading deeper into the woods.

"Here?"

The crow cawed again.

"Thank you," the Bard said, making his way into the darkness.

It didn't take long until the path opened into the forgotten land and there, standing before the Bard was the leafless tree.

"Hello, old friend," he said.

Movement beside the base of the tree caught his attention. He watched with fear as four ghostly apparitions appeared, moving alongside the trunk.

He knew who it was. George and the three sisters.

His love.

There she stood.

"It's time," he said, as three of the shapes evaporated into the gloom.

The last shape motioned, as though it was beckoning the Bard.

It was Sarah.

This he was sure of.

"I'm coming," he whispered, the weight of age leaving.

Two steps towards the tree and his hands returned to their former shape. He could've played his instrument if it was before him. He would've stayed and played for the rest of time.

Instead, he went and sat at the base of the tree.

He closed his eyes.

The Bard would wait until his soul left, and his body grew its own tree.

## END.

# THE TREE (THE WITCH #2) - ABOUT

So, I went back!

As I mentioned in the previous 'about,' I revisited the world. I felt like the ending was ambiguous enough that if you only read that first story – maybe the Bard dies. But maybe he doesn't.

I really wanted to go back and revisit just how deep the Bard and Sarah's love was and how the Bard saw Sarah and Rebecca as people and not as this scary creature with powers.

I also wanted to come back and touch on George, and how his life had went.

I hope 'The Tree' was a fitting finale for that world. I will never say never about returning, but at this stage, I don't believe I will.

I had however released a story in that world, which you can read next.

## WON'T YOU OPEN THE DOOR?

**(Originally published in The Horror Collection:
Silver Edition)**

1.

"Please, won't you open the door?"

The old hag's voice woke him from his sleep. Alexander had stayed awake until the fire had burned down to just coals, but when her wretched voice made its way through the door of the cabin he'd bolted upright, hand finding his rifle automatically.

He cursed the floorboards as they creaked. He wanted to make it to the window nearest the door and look out, confirm he wasn't just hearing things, that she'd come and was outside.

"Won't you please let me in? It's awfully cold and I heard the howl of a wolf."

Her voice had softened but he wasn't so foolish to believe the hag had been replaced by a young lady seeking refuge.

As he neared the door he crouched down to peer underneath. His heart wished that no feet would be visibly and to his surprise there wasn't any.

This made him stop and think. Maybe he *was* imagining the voice?

He shuffled over to the window, keeping his body low, not wanting to be seen.

He took a breath and gripped his rifle, *too tight,* he thought, letting his hands relax. Father, had told him to have soft hands when firing the gun. *"If you're rigid, boy, your aim won't be true."*

He squeezed his eyes shut, then steeled himself to look outside. The night was clear and the moon provided enough light to allow him to view the porch before the door.

Nothing.

No old crone, no young beauty.

*Ah, hell. It had been my mind playing tricks on me,* he thought.

He turned to walk back to his bed. Maybe he'd get the fire up and going again, take the chill off. A noise from the window stole his attention back.

Looking, he saw a decayed finger tapping on the glass. The nail had to be two inches in length and as he watched it tap it began to move in a circular motion. Before he could figure out what was happening the glass fell inward, a perfect circle cut open in its place.

"Won't you open the door, dear?"

He stood, the tapping noise ringing in his ears. He could feel his legs moving, carrying him across the short space between the fireplace and the door. He wanted to yell out and stop himself but he couldn't, the tapping he'd heard holding him in a trance-like stupor.

His hand reached out and he felt the knob turn in his hand, the door unlatch and begin to swing inwards as he pulled it open.

On the porch – the hag.

She was a small lady, maybe five feet at most, but she was hovering two feet off the ground below. She smiled at him, exposing her decayed gums. She had no teeth so when she chuckled her festering tongue lolled around freely.

"You?"

"Such a good boy," she said before lunging at him.

It was over in moments. She feasted on his neck, drinking deep of his blood.

She left his corpse on the floor before disappearing into the woods under the cloudless black sky.

2.

His body was found several days later, when his father and brother came searching. They had planned on coming to visit Alexander, so when they arrived they were shaken.

"It was a witch, father. I have no doubt," young Ezekiel said as they examined the corpse of his sibling. The body had been drained of all of its blood, and while a few critters had come and had a few bits and bites from his flesh, he was otherwise untouched.

"We must bury your brother. Then, we will avenge him."

They each took an end, carrying the body outside. Without life and without blood, they were surprised with how light he was.

Retrieving two shovels, they began to dig.

By midday sweat shone on their foreheads, frequent sleeve wiping was needed to keep their eyes from stinging.

"Father, we could see if brother has any water or food."

Ezekiel used his shovel as a prop, leaning into it while supporting his weight with his arms.

"We will not enter into that cursed place again," the old man replied. "Why look," he pointed to the trees nearby, "even now the trees near this grave have started to turn."

Sure enough, Ezekiel saw the base of each trunk turning black. As he looked closer he spotted movement. Kneeling now to inspect it, he leaned in before suddenly leaping backwards. Dozens of snakes were now birthing from the bark of the tree. The hissing rose in volume as more and more wiggling reptiles pushed forth and fell into a ball on the ground at the base of the tree.

"Back up, boy. This is the work of the devil," Father said. The two retreated from the hole they'd been digging. They watched as the writhing mass made its way to the body before consuming it and then dropping over the edge of the grave.

"Do we fill it in with dirt, father?"

"No. We leave. We leave and we never come back to these miserable grounds again."

They untied their horses, pulling themselves onto the saddles. They took a moment to watch the open grave, ensuring that nothing crawled from it, then Ezekiel waited as his father set fire to the cabin.

The heat of the flames faded quickly as they rode towards home.

3.

Ezekiel dreamed of the snakes for weeks after, but soon the incident was forgotten. He missed his brother greatly, but due to the circumstances surrounding his passing his parents forbid his name from being brought up around the dinner table.

It wasn't until a decade later, when his father passed away, that things from the past made themselves known again.

4.

They decided to follow the family traditions for burying Mr. Thomas. Ezekiel brought the horse and cart to the mortuary. They loaded his dead father's body into a wooden coffin, then slid it onto the deck of the cart. Ezekiel drove the cart down Main Street, clanging the funeral bell every ten seconds. As the cart travelled, mourners fell in behind, walking along until they reached the cemetery.

While the graveyard workers delicately lowered the

casket into the grave, Ezekiel felt his chest tighten. He felt his arms clenching, the nails puncturing the flesh of his palms. He could feel the blood seep out and collect between his fingers before finally it dripped to the ground below. He watched as the sun dimmed and the clouds darkened.

As the priest delivered the eulogy and quoted some bible passages, Ezekiel could swear he saw movement from the walls of the grave. It hit him then – *the trees*. He remembered how snakes had come forth from the trunks of the trees when they'd been digging his brother's grave.

Now, he watched as the dirt started to crumble and oval, oblong shapes started to push their way out of the soil. The workers now noticed what was happening and scrambled out of the hole.

While the rest of the gathered mourners screamed and fled in horror, Ezekiel walked to the edge of his father's grave and watched with shock as hundreds and then thousands of snakes filled the opening.

When they finally broke the ridge and started to slither away, Ezekiel left.

Something had cursed his brother and was passed to his father. Now, as the last living male in the Thomas family, it would pass to him. He decided then, that would have to return to that damned land.

5.

Ezekiel drank himself stupid for a week after his father was buried. He drank to forget and he drank to build up some liquid courage. Whatever was causing this series of events was such that it was making him question his bravery.

He'd asked a few of his friends to aid him, giving them the barest of details. Only his childhood friend, Oliver had agreed to come along. This warmed his heart. Oliver was the most pragmatic person Ezekiel had ever met. This would do them well if anything peculiar was to occur.

Once his headache left and he stopped spilling his guts, he called on Oliver and the two saddled up their horses and turned towards Ezekiel's brother's land.

6.

On the second day of their trip, Oliver began to notice owls. They were flying through the trees, swooping through the sky or simply sitting on branches watching the duo.

"That's not normal behaviour," Oliver mentioned, a shiver running through Ezekiel.

They stopped on the bank of the river to set up camp. They tied the horses up and made a fire, then fashioned a lean-to with some downed branches and a thick blanket.

Ezekiel tossed and turned, the eyes of the owls peppering his dreams.

7.

In the morning, Oliver found that the horses had broken free during the night. Ezekiel questioned that, saying that it looked like the reins had been cut through as he inspected what was left behind.

Either way, that meant they had to make their way on foot now. Oliver chatted about how strange the growth patterns looked of the surrounding forest, while Ezekiel ignored his friend and tried to determine just what his brother had stumbled on.

He thought back to the day when he and his father had found his brother. He hated saying his name, even thinking it was tough, but Alexander had been a great older brother to him and his death still caused him grief.

8.

On the fourth night while the two ate a light dinner and reminisced about their childhood, a scream intruded into the stillness of the surrounding forest.

Both men bolted to their feet, looking in all directions.

"What the hell was that?" Oliver asked, his face as white as a sheet.

"Damned if I know," Ezekiel replied. They circled the edge of the campfire light, trying to see if someone was near. With no luck they returned to the warmth by the flames.

"I ain't going to be sleeping tonight," Oliver tried to joke, but Ezekiel didn't laugh in reply. Instead he was fixated on the path they'd arrived on.

"Someone just ran across that trail, up there," he said, pointing down the way.

"You sure?"

"Yup," he replied. He sat and stared for what felt like

an eternity, watching to see if the figure darted across again.

His eyes finally betrayed him and sleep took over. Oliver followed soon behind.

As the two men's heads dropped to their chest and soft snores started, a sickly figure stood in the pathway. It lurched forward, towards the duo, feet scuffing the ground, entrails dragging behind it.

When it made it to the edge of the light it stopped and let out another god-awful scream.

Ezekiel and Oliver woke with a start, finding that whatever had made the noise had disappeared into the forest.

9.

"Ok, level with me," Oliver said the next morning as they approached the edge of Ezekiel's brother's land. "What's really going on here?"

"Some*thing* killed my brother and my father. I think whatever it was has cursed my family. It passed between them. Now, I need to stop it, before it stops me."

Oliver stood expressionless. Ezekiel could see the wheels turning as he processed the information.

"Right."

"I swear on my life. Did you not see what happened at my father's funeral?" He asked. He knew Oliver had personally witnessed the arrival of the snakes.

"That same thing happened when we were burying Alexander. Snakes began to birth from the surrounding trees. It got to the point that me and father torched my brother's cabin and fled."

Oliver solemnly nodded, unease growing throughout his body.

After a few more paces Ezekiel realized that he was walking alone. He turned to find Oliver standing on the roadway. When Ezekiel approached he found his friend was shaking, eyes wet with tears ready to flee down his cheeks.

"Oliver, are you ok?"

"I'm afraid I've pissed myself," he replied.

Ezekiel put a hand on his shoulder, squeezing the man firmly.

"If you need to return home, I won't judge you any less. I would appreciate the help and your companionship. Truth be told, I've never been this afraid in my life. I would understand if you departed."

Oliver shook his head.

"No. A friend needs me. You've been my dearest friend since as long as I can remember. You'd never abandon me. I apologize for my current state, but I will continue."

They shook hands and carried on.

After some time, Ezekiel decided to ask Oliver some pointed questions.

"Oliver. Do you believe in the devil?"

"I can't say I do, Ezekiel. While I am a firm believer in God and the word of the bible, I don't believe that there is a single figure out there, waiting to capture wayward souls."

Ezekiel took in what his friend had said, then asked his

next question.

"What about demons and witches?"

As he asked the question a dozen ravens cawed before swooping down at the duo. They ducked and rolled on the dirt, trying to stay out of range from their talons.

"Run!" Ezekiel said as the birds regrouped, turning to swarm the men.

Oliver took off at a dead sprint, his leather shoes slapping hard against the ground. Ezekiel did his best to keep up, but the birds were faster.

He felt their sharp beaks start hitting his exposed neck, causing him to summersault and then tumble out of control. When he finally stopped he looked around, finding the birds had turned their wrath onto Oliver. His friend was trying to bat them away with a branch he'd found, swinging at the ravens as they dive-bombed him over and over.

As Ezekiel searched for another stick to help his friend, he saw one of the black bastards swoop in and viciously claw his face. His cheek opened up and blood began to spurt out.

Oliver dropped his branch and took off running again. As Ezekiel arrived where his friend had been, the ravens appeared to have lost interest, deciding to turn and fly away, leaving him standing there holding a stick.

"Oliver! They've gone," he yelled, running after him.

He caught up to him a short distance later, Oliver sitting on the side of the path. He was holding a hand to his face and Ezekiel could see blood had made its way in between his fingers.

"It hurts. It hurts and it burns," he said as Ezekiel

jogged up to him.

Ezekiel inspected his wound. He found the edges to be bubbling and the skin looked burned, as though Oliver had been doused with acid. His hand was the same.

"Those ravens. Whatever they were, they weren't normal birds," Oliver said then. "To answer your question, I don't believe in demons or witches. Look at the foolishness over in Salem. But, I do believe in evil as a power. I can't fully rationalize it and say *why*, just that I firmly believe a person can harness it and do bad with it. I think this is one of those times."

Ezekiel gave Oliver his handkerchief, letting his friend use it to put pressure on his cheek. It looked like the wound was getting worse minute by minute.

"If you're still up for it, I say we try and cover more ground. We might be able to make the location where Alexander's cabin was before dark."

Oliver got up and they continued on.

Behind them, the forest closed over the pathway, making it appear as though it had never been there at all.

10.

When they arrived at the edge of his brother's property, Ezekiel paused.

"Look at the trees," he said to Oliver, pointing to the forest edge around them. Alexander had spent a half decade harvesting the land, removing growth with plans for a farm and a large garden. The trees now all had holes throughout them, from the ground to about five feet up. The two men could see through the holes, as though someone had drilled straight through with a piece of metal.

"Those are from snakes. I know it," Ezekiel meekly said, wishing those words didn't exist. All around the bases of the trees they could see where things had slithered away, the leaves pushed into thin paths.

"Wherever they went, I'm glad. It means they ain't here," Oliver quipped as he stepped forward into the opening. Ezekiel found that he couldn't take that step. That he was against an invisible barrier that was preventing him from moving ahead.

"You coming?"

Ezekiel nodded and forced his feet forward, feeling his body shiver as he crossed the property threshold.

Oliver was walking faster now, Ezekiel not sure why. When his friend arrived at the top of the short hill, he turned, his face contorted with confusion.

"I thought you said you guys burned your brother's cabin down?"

When Ezekiel arrived beside Oliver, he was dumbfounded.

There it was. The cabin. As good as new.

"I don't understand? Father torched it."

Oliver strode confidently to the building, while Ezekiel took his time.

Nothing about this scenario felt natural. Ezekiel could feel his skin crawl and the hair on his arms stand at attention the closer he got to the house. It was as though an energy was being transmitted from the cabin, an energy that only he could feel.

Oliver appeared to not notice it. He walked directly to

the front door. Looking at his friend, he knocked once and when the door opened, he stepped inside with a smile on his face. The door slammed shut behind him and a scream came from within. Ezekiel rushed forward, pounding on the door, kicking at the hinges, trying desperately to get inside. He grabbed the door knob, feeling the metal burn into his palm. He yelled in pain, but didn't pull away. He needed to get inside, needed to save his friend.

The screaming reached an ear-shattering pitch, before coming to a sudden end. Ezekiel stepped away from the door, not wanting to look inside, but drawn to the window by the door.

He noticed scratch marks on the surface of the glass. He didn't want to know what made them, instead he blocked it from his mind as he looked through.

There, sitting on a chair by the fire was Oliver.

Ezekiel tried the door, finding it open with ease. Stepping into the cabin, he was met with the aroma of fresh baked bread and coffee.

"Ah, Ezekiel, I was wondering when you'd catch up," Oliver said.

Rubbing his eyes and smacking his face, Ezekiel looked at his friend.

"How is this possible? I heard you scream in agony? Even your face is healed." Ezekiel looked at his own palms, finding no burns on them as well.

Oliver walked to his friend and gave him a once over, concern on his face.

"Are you ok, Ezekiel? Dehydrated? What happened to my face?"

Ezekiel wasn't sure what to believe now. He sat down, feeling the exhaustion in his muscles as he let his legs splay out before him.

Oliver brought him a cup of coffee, steam coming off the liquid.

"Thank you, very kind," he said, accepting the drink.

"I'm going to prepare some dinner. Then I think we can both use a good night's sleep," his friend replied, heading to the kitchen area.

Ezekiel had two deep drinks of his coffee before the hazy arrival of slumber started to bob his head. *I should get up and help Oliver*, he thought as his eyes closed and he slumped sideways.

In the kitchen his friend's eyes glowed red and a grin spread wide on his face.

11.

Ezekiel woke up some time during the night. He found himself naked in bed, unsure of how he got there or when he got there. He looked around the darkened room and recognized it as being his brother's old room. At one time Alexander was going to expand the cabin and add a second floor, but found it too difficult to accomplish on his own. So there was still the beginning of some stairs along the one wall, which always seemed weird to Ezekiel. Why hadn't his brother ever removed them?

He heard a rhythmic swishing noise coming from the living area. He could make out the red glow of flames from the fire pit through the open doorway. Not bothering to get dressed, he walked to the door and looked out.

The scene before him made him cover his mouth, not wanting a scream to grab unwanted attention.

Oliver was kneeling before the fire. Standing beside him was a rail-thin woman. Both were naked. Her belly was distended, hanging down over her crotch. From where he stood, Ezekiel could see movement below her skin, as though something was trying to push its way out. The swishing noise was the sound of the hag using her thickened nails to intricately slice back row upon row of Oliver's skin. She'd already stripped his right side and was now working on his left side. The skin hung from his muscles like string from a balloon.

The woman was humming as she sliced into Oliver again, dragging her nail down his back. Then she grasped the top of the strip and tugged it away as she pulled it down, draping it below.

Ezekiel felt the room grow dizzy, his knees shaking and buckling. He was going to vomit but couldn't focus on anything.

"Ah, Ezekiel. So glad you could join us," the crone spoke.

The room spun to black and Ezekiel felt his impact on the floor. His vision spun, the last thing he saw was her crusted feet walking towards him.

12.

"Breakfast is ready."

Oliver's voice brought him from his sleep.

Ezekiel swung his legs from the bed, stood and stretched.

He felt refreshed.

Joining Oliver in the kitchen, he saw some boiled potatoes on a plate with some eggs.

"Thank you," he said, taking his plate.

"How did you sleep?" Oliver asked, before taking a drink.

"I had horrible dreams. Awful dreams. Oddly, I feel refreshed. Rejuvenated. You?"

Oliver smiled, sipping some more of his drink.

"Never better," he replied, setting the cup down. "Never better."

13.

The day was spent inspecting the property. Oliver suggested they stay together, telling Ezekiel that he didn't feel comfortable on his own.

They found all of the trees to be the same – holes bored through. In the farthest corner of the property they found hundreds of shed snake skins. When Oliver stooped down and picked some up, they disintegrated, blowing away like dust.

While returning to the cabin, Ezekiel spotted something through the trees. Motioning to his friend, they stepped off the property and into the forest, wanting to inspect what had caught his eye.

There on a fallen tree were the displayed skeletons of a dozen owls and a dozen ravens.

Oliver called for his friend to come see something. Against his better judgement, Ezekiel went and when he arrived he wished he'd turned and walked to the cabin instead.

The talons of the last raven were caked in dried blood. As Oliver stood, his cheek opened up again, the flap of skin making a slapping noise as it flopped open and connected with his face.

"We need to leave," he said calmly, as though he was looking at something completely different than Ezekiel.

The two made their way back to the cabin. They stopped at the front door, sharing a panicked look. The door was open.

"You closed it, yes?" Ezekiel asked.

"Of course, we both waited while I bolted it, remember?"

Ezekiel did, which made this discovery all the more concerning.

Upon entering they saw the place was in disarray, as though a lawman had ransacked their residence, looking for contraband.

"Who did this?" Oliver asked, still paying no mind to his exposed cheek.

Ezekiel didn't have an answer. Instead they closed and barricaded the door. They spent the rest of the day returning the living quarters to some sort of order.

As the sun began to descend towards setting, Ezekiel felt dread pulse through his veins.

"Oliver. Promise me, promise me that we won't go to sleep. Promise me that the two of us will stay awake until morning. Once the sun rises, we'll run back as fast as we can. We'll get a priest and we'll let them cleanse these lands."

Oliver nodded, eyes staring vacantly ahead.

14.

It had been dark for a few hours when there was three loud knocks on the door.

The two men had remained sitting near the fire in silent thought, each keeping watch on the other.

"Please, won't you open the door?"

A voice as old as time spoke through the wood, through the barricade.

Ezekiel jumped to his feet. Oliver joined him and the two watched the door, expecting the wood to burst inward.

"Oliver? Ezekiel? Please let me in, it's so very cold." The voice that spoke was now the voice of Alexander. Oliver had to grab his friend, hold him back.

"That's not your brother," he said, firmly.

Three more forceful knocks on the door.

"Let me in you ungrateful boy," the voice of Ezekiel's father bellowed.

Oliver crept to the window beside the door. When he finally looked out, Ezekiel watched as his friend's body went rigid. He turned to Ezekiel, color drained from his face.

"She's floating," he said.

Then the window exploded, glass slicing into Oliver's head. The top of his scalp was cut open, peeling his hair back. A rotting hand entered through the jagged opening and ripped Oliver's head from his neck.

The body slumped to the floor as the head was pulled into the darkness outside.

"Oh, I'll come in. One way or another. Just you wait," the hag called out.

Ezekiel grabbed the iron fire poker and held it out before him. He shuffled forward, making his way to the body of his friend. Keeping his distance he looked outside. The front porch was clear, the hag having fled.

He went back and sat on his chair by the fire. He vowed to stay awake, to not fall asleep. Soon, the adrenaline caught up and he began to crash. As his head bobbed and his eyes fought to stay open he caught a glimpse of movement by the window.

Squinting, he saw Oliver's head had been impaled on a shard of broken glass. As he fell asleep he saw his friend's detached head lick its lips.

15.

The rumbling of his stomach signalled it was time for Ezekiel to wake up. He found he was back in bed, once again having no recollection of how he made it there.

Looking out through the window in the room, he found the sun was beginning to set. He'd slept through the entire day.

Entering the living area, he found that during his sleep Oliver's body had been snatched, a trail of blood showing where it had been dragged through the broken window. Peering outside, he could follow the blood pathway all the way to the edge of the trees. There he found Oliver's body, strung up by his innards between two dying birch.

"What do you want?" Ezekiel yelled into the black.

His question was answered by three hard knocks on

STEVE STRED

the door, causing him to jump back away from the window.

"All I want, is for you to open the door," the woman's voice replied.

Behind him the fire erupted, flames dancing high and wide from the hearth. Ezekiel looked in horror as the blaze caught the wood surrounding, the cabin beginning to burn.

"I lived on these lands, raised my kids here. Grew old and was happy. Then that Alexander comes along and takes what wasn't his. All I wanted was to rest in peace. Buried here in this land, *my* land, but instead your brother digs up my bones and desecrates my grave."

It all clicked then. His brother had stolen this property. Now the family was paying.

"I'm sorry. I'm so sorry. I don't know why Alexander did that," he cried, dropping to his knees.

"Your apology means nothing. If you won't open the door, then you can stay inside and burn."

Ezekiel got to his feet and rushed to the door, trying to open it. He found it was immoveable. He tried pulling it and turning it, but no amount of effort would budge it. He then went to the broken window to try and climb out but found the crone had barricaded the opening from the outside, heavy logs stacked up against the cabin.

He could hear her laughing from beyond the door.

The flames grew hotter and higher, his clothes now burning. His skin bubbled, blistered and burst.

As the yard beyond the house whistled with the arrival of thousands of snakes a pained scream could be heard from inside the inferno.

The lady made her way to the edge of the forest, pausing to listen to Ezekiel's final sounds, before disappearing into the blackness beyond.

16.

When Ezekiel and Oliver didn't return, his friends sent out a search party. For two weeks they searched to no avail, unable to find a trace of the duo.

Making it all the more difficult was that where the path should have been, most of it was now grown over or appeared to have never existed. The group had to slash through underbrush and chop down trees to make any progress.

Finally, after making it to Alexander's former property, they found two graves. One had a small stone with the letter 'A' crudely carved into it, which they believed to be Alexander's. The other grave had a plank of wood placed on it. The name 'Lauren' was scratched into the surface.

The group said some last rites for the two, then saddled up and started the journey back to town.

When they left the edge of the property, they heard the familiar sounds of owl's hooting from the forest.

They didn't see the rotting, head-less remains of Oliver's body in the trees or the burned corpse of Ezekiel draped over a rock just off the pathway as they rode.

END

## WON'T YOU OPEN THE DOOR? -
## ABOUT

As of writing this, I've released a number of works and been featured in a number of anthologies. But there was a time where I only received rejections for my work. I'd put it at around 200 rejections before I decided to just focus on being a better writer and keep releasing my own works. David Sodergren has always been instrumental in my improvements as a writer, from his beta reads, to his copy-editing to just feedback in general.

I was using drabbles as a way to be more efficient with storytelling and to my surprise, I finally had my first acceptance from Kevin J. Kennedy for his '100 Word Horrors 3.' This was followed by another acceptance in his '100 Word Horrors 4.' I was stunned.

Imagine my absolute shock when he then sent me an invite to submit something for his 'The Horror Collection' series.

I decided to revamp the hag story I was working on,

expand it and submit and Kevin loved it! 'Won't You Open the Door,' is more of a back story in the world of 'The Witch' telling a tale of earlier terror in the area.

As a side note – the character of the hag was named after a bookish friend I made through Instagram! Cheers, Lauren!

8

## THE ASSISTANT

A t sixteen, Kyle was finally allowed to start working in the family funeral home.

"A boy's gotta know a hard day's work," his grandpa would say, stitching up a body for viewing. Kyle never understood his grandpa giving him a hard time about working. He desired to work, but legally he wasn't allowed.

It hadn't always been that way.

Kyle grew up afraid of the basement.

Down there. That was where the bodies were. Where the tools to open them up and clean them out and preserve them were. The chemicals and fluids and powders and stuff.

But at twelve, that fear began to turn to curiosity and at fourteen a morbid curiosity.

He would visit more often, ask more questions.

*"How did they die?"*

*"How old were they?"*

Things that he wanted to know; he'd ask.

The more engrossed he grew with the business the more the bullies at school singled him out. He didn't care. In a small town like this, he knew that sooner or later he'd be prepping his classmates for burial.

Now, on his sixteenth birthday, he was thrown into the deep end on day one. A car crash happened on the outskirts of town, one deceased. The driver was transported from the hospital to the funeral home where preparations would be made for their service.

"Come down, Kyle, transports arrived," his dad called up the stairs. Kyle cleaned up after dinner quickly before he bounced down the stairs, a bit surprised at the level of excitement that had grown within.

His grandpa was backing the hearse into the loading bay, his dad directing him through the mirrors. Once the vehicle parked, the bay door lowered, and his dad opened the swinging back door of the hearse.

A body bag was on the stretcher, the deceased hidden from view, for now.

"I thought you brought the bodies from the morgue in the refrigerated van?"

"We usually do," his dad replied, helping to pull the stretcher out. "But the van's still in the shop and the family wants a quick turnaround for viewing."

Kyle helped guide the stretcher down the hall to the prep area, nervous about the bag being opened. *What would be under that layer of material?* He ran a thousand scenarios through his mind as they locked the wheels and he grabbed one end, while his dad grabbed the other.

"1, 2, 3" he counted, before they hefted the body off the stretcher and onto the stainless-steel table.

"You want to do the honors?" his dad asked.

Kyle looked from his dad to his grandpa and understood that it was a family rite of passage. That these two had been waiting for this moment for sixteen years.

He adjusted his gloves, then tentatively reached forward and grasped the zipper. Slowly he pulled it along the side of the bag, down the length of the table, before coming to the end. He grabbed the flap of the bag and pulled it across, exposing the body.

An unfamiliar woman lay before the three men. Kyle's dad looked at the paperwork sent along, flipping the pages back and forth.

"Odd," he finally said. "Listed as a Jane Doe. Had no ID on her, no paperwork in the car that they could find, and the car didn't have a license plate."

"I thought you said the family wanted a quick turn-around?" Kyle's grandpa said.

"That was the message relayed to me by the coroner."

"Any next of kin listed?"

"Nope," his dad said, flipping the pages again.

"How strange. In any case, we have a work order here. Let's get this young woman prepped and presentable. Kyle, you want to do the honors again?" Grandpa extended his arms, scissor handles pointed in his direction.

Kyle froze. They wanted him to cut her clothes off. He hadn't even thought about the fact he'd be seeing someone naked so soon, let alone a woman.

"I... uh..." he cleared his throat, face growing red, "sure, I mean, yes... yes."

He took the scissors and looked back at the body. His dad and grandpa began to chuckle, before it grew into full blown laughter.

Kyle didn't understand. He struggled to find anything funny about his nervousness or the situation.

"She's wearing an old dress, you dolt," his dad finally said, grinning at Kyle.

*Of course*, he thought, *no need to cut the dress off.*

"Come here, give me a hand," his grandpa said, grabbing the woman under her arms and lifting her upper body off the table. "Grab the bottom of her dress and pull it up."

Kyle grabbed the hem of the dress and began to pull it up towards grandpa's arms. She wore no shoes, which was what Kyle noticed first, but when he looked at her feet closer, he stopped.

"What is it?"

He looked at his dad, then his grandpa, then back at her feet.

"She has no toenails."

The three leaned in, grandpa still holding her in a position not so far from the Heimlich manoeuvre. They examined her muddy, dirty feet. It had been a long time since she'd last showered or bathed, but sure enough, she had no nails. Thick scabs sat in place of them.

"Jesus. Haven't seen that before. At least I don't think so. Seen a lot of crazy shit," his grandpa said, hefting her up again. "Come on now, pull her dress up."

Kyle grabbed the bottom of the material again and

continued to pull it up. He bunched it up as his dad grabbed the dress while Kyle and his grandpa did a strange dance of moving and holding her so that the dress was able to be pulled over her chest, her shoulders and then over her head. Once she was nude, his grandpa delicately returned her to the table.

The three stood in shocked silence at her body.

The torso and chest were criss-crossed with scars, no rhyme or reason as to the directions they travelled. She had ample breasts, even laying down, but they had not been spared. Her left breast was missing its nipple, a jagged wound left behind suggesting it had been bitten or ripped off. Her right breast had burn marks and dark holes. His grandpa reached out and poked one hole with a finger, inserting the tip. He looked at the other two, eyebrows high.

Her legs had large gashes on the inside of her thighs, as though someone had been slowly stripping her flesh away, a section at a time.

Her dense pubic hair covered any trauma that may have happened there, but Kyle felt queasy even thinking what would be uncovered if it was to be shaved off.

"Look here," his dad said, inspecting her hands. "Her nails are missing from her hands."

"I don't feel right about this," grandpa said. "Things don't add up. We've worked on abused women before, but this was sadistic torture. Purposeful. I need a minute." He walked to the door, stripping his gloves off and discarding them in the garbage can. He looked from his son to his grandson one more time before exiting the room.

"You ever see any of this before?" he asked his dad.

"No. Honestly. Never."

Kyle wasn't sure what he was supposed to do. He wanted to pick something up, or clean or whatever, just something so that he was doing anything. The body had this odd energy that was creeping him out.

"Dad, maybe we just leave the body overnight and finish in the morning?"

"Can't. Work order says transport will be here at nine."

"They're not having a service here?"

"No, not this time. Body is being transported to..." he grabbed the paperwork again and flipped through it, "huh. No destination listed. Everything about this is odd. No matter. We have a job to do and we do it with pride."

His dad went over, going through the prep checklist, getting the tools laid out on the tray beside the table. This time, he didn't ask Kyle if he wanted to make any cuts or incisions, instead, he made the first cut to get a line in and start getting the body ready.

As fluid went in and fluid came out, Kyle had the first inkling he was going to throw up. He looked around, desperately, for the nearest bowl, not sure if he'd make it to the garbage can by the door.

"Head upstairs, Kyle," his dad said, never looking up at him.

"Thanks," he replied hastily, as he rushed from the room.

KYLE WAITED PATIENTLY, sitting on the couch in the living room. He expected his dad to come upstairs at some point and give him grief for leaving.

When the door to the basement opened and closed, he found he was holding his breath, waiting for a storm to arrive.

"You OK?" his dad asked. He was standing in the entry way between the kitchen and the living room, holding a beer.

Kyle gave a nod, heard his dad approach. He looked up, surprised to see a beer presented to him from his dad. Kyle looked from the beer his dad, to the beer and back again, unsure if this was a trick.

"Go ahead, you've earned it."

Kyle accepted it, feeling the cold condensation from the bottle transfer to his palm. His dad popped the top off with the bottle opener and then clinked his bottle to Kyle's.

"Cheers."

"Cheers," Kyle replied, taking a delicate sip. He'd never tasted alcohol before, let alone had his dad offer one. It was cold but tasted good. He took a second, longer drink, his dad smirking.

"So, I'll ask again. You OK?"

"Yeah. Sorry."

"Nothing to be sorry about. It's a lot the first time you're in there *actually* doing the work. Very different than when you'd pop your head in and ask questions. I saw your color fading fast. Was surprised you made it past the *'getting her nude'* stage," he said, chuckling.

He gave his dad a smile, embarrassment still his main emotion.

"Seriously, Kyle. Don't sweat it. I've got her done to stage where you can sleep on it tonight. Tomorrow morning, we'll be up bright and early, and we can finish things off before pick-up. Sound good?"

"Sounds good."

"OK. Go grab some sleep. I'll wake you in the morning."

———

AT FIRST, Kyle thought it was his dad shaking him awake.

As he struggled to open his eyes, he found his room to still be dark, with the outside world matching.

"Huh? Wha...?" he asked to the empty room.

As he sat up, his bed rocked again, as though from a force underneath it.

*"Come,"* a voice whispered to him, drawing his attention to the hallway outside his room.

*"Come,"* it said again, beckoning him into the kitchen.

*"Down here,"* it sang to him, from behind the closed door leading to the basement.

Kyle grasped the door handle, surprised when he found it not to be burning hot or freezing cold. That was the air that was waiting for him upon opening the door though. He noticed the temperature drop as he made his way tentatively down the stairs. Arriving at the door to the prep room, he found he didn't want to open the door.

*"Please, come in,"* the voice replied, as though hearing his thoughts.

Entering, he flipped the light switch, watching as the fluorescent lighting illuminated the dark space.

He had expected to be staring at a body on the table with its organs removed and fluids going in and out.

Instead, Kyle was staring at an empty prep table and the feeling that he was being watched.

"Hello?"

A shuffle came from the back corner, shadows offering just enough protection from the light.

"Hey, I know you're the dead woman. Why did you call for me?"

Kyle knew he should be terrified. The woman was dead, there was no debating that. She'd suffered horrific wounds and then was in a car accident. But, for some odd reason, he had no fear.

*"Can I trust you?"* she asked from the dark.

"Yeah, yeah of course."

*"How can I be sure?"*

"Uh... I don't know? I don't have a gun or anything," he replied, lifting his hands up by his sides to show her they were empty.

He saw her move closer to where the light reached.

*"Please. You must help me. I need to be free."*

"You're dead?"

*"To you I may appear dead, but I am far from."*

"What do you need me to do?"

*"I need you to create a path from where I stand to the grass outside with sand."*

"With sand? Where am I supposed to get sand? It's the middle of the night and we don't live at the beach."

He heard a scraping sound and her hushed whispers.

A wind whirled around his legs and when he looked, there beside him was a large bucket filled with sand.

*"Now, begin."*

It was a command that squeezed deep down into his insides. He didn't look at her, instead he simply grabbed the scoop that lay at the top and began sprinkling the sand as best he could.

He made it to the doorway, before glancing towards the dark edge where she'd been standing. He saw her in the shadows, nude, on all fours. Her feet and hands had changed; her hands possessed long claws; her feet shaped like talons.

*"Continue,"* she directed, still not moving into the light.

He did as told.

When he reached the door at the end of the hall, that opened into their small backyard, he propped it open with the rock they kept, just for that purpose and looked back.

Kyle wished he hadn't.

Her face had transformed as well.

Her jaw hung low and had elongated, a thick serpentine tongue swishing back and forth as though searching for prey. Her eyes blazed red in the dim lighting. She continued forward on all fours, reminding Kyle of a proud lion showing off a kill.

He continued creating the sand path, until he was a few feet from the grass. He'd been afraid that he'd wake up his dad, so he'd not moved any of the outdoor chairs on the cement pad. Instead, the path snaked around the various obstacles. Kyle stopped and stepped onto the grass, watching as the woman-thing arrived at the end of the sand.

*"Another scoop,"* she said, her eyes boring a hole into his.

"Not until you tell me what you are."

Kyle found he couldn't fully see her; it was as though his eyes were unable to focus on any one part of her.

*"I am something you shouldn't question,"* she responded.

Kyle went to speak, but she snapped her fingers, her two claws clacking together, and he found he was unable to speak, let alone open his mouth. Panic gripped him immediately, before he realized he'd dropped the scoop and sand had landed in the empty pass, finalizing the path to the grass.

"Thank you," the woman said.

As soon as she touched the grass, her body shimmered, and Kyle cried into his shut mouth as she disappeared into thin air.

"Kyle?"

It was his dad calling to him from inside the house.

"I'm out here," he replied, surprising himself with the return of his voice and ability to speak.

"What's going on, son?"

He looked at him with great worry, troubled to find Kyle outside.

"Something's happened. You'll never believe me, but something's happened."

"What? Tell me, I'll give it my best try."

"She's gone."

"Who? The dead woman?"

His dad turned and started walking to the prep room, but Kyle knew that he would find the table bare.

## END.

## THE ASSISTANT - ABOUT

I wrote this story a while back but during the first go wasn't sure how to end it. I got to the point of the woman whispering for Kyle to come to the prep room.

Then I was stuck.

I finally tackled it again recently, and found that it had a nice flow once I had a solid idea of how I wanted to end it.

I've always loved the autopsy aspect of horror, both in books and movies, where layers are peeled back and more is discovered. After reading through this, I found a very distinct 'The Autopsy of Jane Doe' vibe. If you haven't watched that movie, I highly recommend it!

# AFTERWORD

Well another offering in the world of Steve Stred has come to an end.

Big thanks to Miranda for the foreword and the amazing artwork. I'll keep bugging her to get her stories finished up and released soon enough! I'd especially love to read the story of The Hairy Woman.

Collections seem to be hit or miss for fans of dark fiction. On the reviewing side, I get burned out on them, but I do love reading them. I'll usually have three-five books on the go, so adding a collection/anthology to offset the longer reads can be a nice break. On the writing side, I actually enjoy writing short fiction. I find it a way to take pieces of ideas that I can't work into longer reads but still can adjust and release it as short stories so that the idea that festered in my brain still has a proper birth.

"Of Witches…" came about from wanting to dive

into a witch piece of fiction, but realizing I had more than one idea sitting there and clanging around in my head.

I'm forever grateful for anyone who reads any of my work. Even more so if you are kind enough to leave a rating or review.

Thank you to all my book community friends who work hard to bring positivity into the world every day!

Big thanks to Mason McDonald for your friendship and cover help!

Thanks to David Sodergren for your friendship and for making me a better writer.

Cheers to Gavin and Kendall Reviews for your tireless work in supporting me, but also so many other authors who frequently are overlooked.

Thanks to Ross Jeffery for your friendship and formatting help.

Thank you to JH Moncrieff for your friendship. It means the world.

Thanks to Duncan Ralston, Justin M. Woodward, RJ Roles, Andrew Cull, Laurel Hightower, Sonora Taylor, Richard Gerlach, Michael Patrick Hicks, and so many others in the community who always have time for a question!

To all the other authors out there who inspire me, thank you!

To the LOHF crew and the Grant gang, cheers for everything you do day in and day out! One day, the goal of having a positive community every day will come, you'll see!

Lastly, to Amanda, Auryn and OJ – you make me the luckiest person alive!

Until we meet again,
Steve
Edmonton, Alberta
July 30, 2020

## ABOUT THE AUTHOR

Steve Stred writes dark, bleak horror fiction.

Steve is the author of number of novels, novellas and collections.

He is proud to work with the Ladies of Horror Fiction to facilitate the Annual LOHF Writers Grant.

Steve is also a voracious reader, reviewing everything he reads and submitting the majority of his reviews to be featured on Kendall Reviews.

Steve Stred is based in Edmonton, AB, Canada and lives with his wife, his son and their dog OJ.

Website: stevestredauthor.wordpress.com
Twitter: @stevestred
Instagram: @stevestred

## MIRANDA CRITES

Miranda Crites is a reader, writer, book reviewer, photographer, artist, and lover of horror from the ghostly woods of rural West Virginia.

The writing bug bit Miranda at a very early age, in fact she was pretty much born with a pen and camera in her hands.

She won the young writers' contest in first grade and received her first camera as a gift when she was nine years old. She has a diploma in Writing for Children and Teenagers although most of her current work is horror fiction and poetry. She is one of "The Thirty," a group of thirty authors who each took a turn in writing a chapter of a horror novel.

Miranda is a member of Kendall Reviews where you can find her horror book reviews and her monthly feature, Miranda Snaps, which generally contains horror fiction and photography.

You can follow Miranda on:
Instagram @Miranda_C_rites
Twitter @Miranda_C_rites
www.mirandacritesreadsandwrites.com

Printed in Dunstable, United Kingdom